Pre-Publication Advance Praise for
DEATH IN THE FLOWERY KINGDOM

I never thought I would enjoy this book. I'm not particularly interested in life in China in ~~1930s and just did not think~~ it would hold my attention.

I WAS WRONG!

GREAT JOB - AGAIN!

—CN, Connecticut

What people are saying about
NO PLACE TO HIDE:

NO PLACE TO HIDE is a tense, beautifully sculpted novel that blends international politics, the military, and of course crime. . . .When an author is able to strike a chord of fear with the opening lines, the reader can be assured the designated genre of 'suspense novel' is correct. Steve does this with direct ease. . . . . And [after this opening], we're off and running and that [fast, tense] pace is sustained throughout this fine book. . . .Reading this second installment of the Trace Austin series develops a need to read the entire series — and that is a solid sign that Steven M. Roth is a novelist of significance.

—Grady Harp, AMAZON HALL OF
FAME TOP 100 REVIEWER

What people are saying about
NO SAFE PLACE:

Steven Roth has written a terrifyingly real bioweapon suspense novel. He has the chops to keep a reader turning pages and anxious about what comes next. *No Safe Place* alerts us to what the government has done and may still be doing to an unsuspecting and unconcerned public. Highly recommended.

—Charlie Stella
Author of *TOMMY RED* and eight other crime novels

What people are saying about
MANDARIN YELLOW

A splendidly told and sophisticated tale by a first-time novelist. The multi-layered murder mystery not only remains engaging throughout, but also offers the reader a superb primer on Chinese culture and history, particularly post-World War II history.

If you're a mystery fan, you shouldn't miss this novel that features a Parker Duofold (the eponymous Mandarin Yellow). This is prime mystery: well plotted and compellingly written. Roth weaves a taut storyline, paces it perfectly, and wraps it in twists and turns that make no sense until you get to the end (when everything clicks perfectly into place). Along the way, he slips in all the clues you need to solve the mystery right along with hero Socrates Cheng.

STEVEN M. ROTH

DEATH
IN THE
FLOWERY
KINGDOM

DEATH
IN THE
FLOWERY
KINGDOM

A 1930s Shanghai Murder Mystery

STEVEN M. ROTH

BLACKSTONE PRESS
A CRIME BOOK IMPRINT

OTHER NOVELS BY STEVEN M. ROTH

Socrates Cheng Mystery Series:
MANDARIN YELLOW
THE MOURNING WOMAN
THE COUNTERFEIT TWIN

Trace Austin Suspense/Thriller Series:
NO SAFE PLACE
NO PLACE TO HIDE

1930s-Shanghai Mystery Series:
DEATH IN THE FLOWERY KINGDOM

Children's Mystery Book:
THE MYSTERY OF THE MISSING DONUT
A Mystery Introducing Owen Roth, Boy Detective

───◆───

With Owen M. Roth
THE DOG WHO PLAYED CENTERFIELD
A Baseball Story

Published by Blackstone Press, a Crime Book Imprint

Cover design by Streetlight Graphics, LLC

ISBN 978-1-7328748-0-0 [Print]

Visit the author's website: http://www.StevenMRoth.com

Shanghai, the whore of the Orient

—Anonymous

DEFINITION: *FLOWER-SELLER GIRL*

1930s Shanghainese slang for a prostitute. Flower-seller girls sometimes also were referred to by the British and Americans in Shanghai as *sing-song girls*.

CHAPTER 1

"Y OU'RE UNDER ARREST, AUNTIE," I said to the coolie woman, addressing her with the customary title we Chinese use when speaking to an elderly woman who is a stranger.

This was not going to be one of my better nights.

Some days — most of the time, in fact — I love being a policeman. Specifically, I love being a member of the Special Branch of the Shanghai Municipal Police Force [SMP], being an inspector detective on the SMP. Other days, at times like this evening, I'm not so sure. On nights like tonight, nights when I'm presented with the opportunity to make an arrest at the Baby Wall, the job seems to me to be bad *joss* — *bad fortune*. But I do my job nevertheless. That's what the SMP pays me to do.

I am called Sun-jin. My full name, to be accurate, is Ling Sun-jin. I am the second-oldest brother of five sons, and am older than our two sisters, who are the youngest siblings in our Ling clan of seven children.

I was standing alone in a thicket of rare huanghuali trees, close by the Garden Bridge, near the place where the muddy Whangpoo River and Soochow Creek come together after flowing past the Bund and the Public Garden. From my hiding place among the trees, I was watching the Baby Wall where some parents come in the night to abandon their newborns, placing them in a pull-down drawer known as the Baby Drawer.

I detested this part of my job, but enforcing the laws of Shanghai is what I do. I am, as I said, a plainclothes inspector detective with the city's police agency whose jurisdiction oversees law enforcement in the combined British and American territory known as the International Settlement.

The year 1935 is a time in our city's history when crime in Shanghai is so unrestrained and so violent that no sane constable- patrolman ever goes out alone after dark to patrol his beat. Nevertheless, as an inspector detective, in spite of the inherent danger in our city, I prefer to work alone, without a partner to encumber me. Fortunately, I no longer patrol a beat.

Most violent crimes in Shanghai are committed by the Chinese. The British and the Americans tend to commit fraud and other monetary crimes. The Japanese rarely commit any crimes, but when they do, they tend to commit non-violent crimes, and almost always do so within their own sub-territory, in the Hongkew section of the International Settlement, north of Soochow Creek, along the Whangpoo River.

As I stood in the damp cold of the early evening, just before sunset, and watched the Baby Wall from within the copse of trees, I heard a noise behind me. Or, perhaps, I merely sensed movement, and thought I heard a noise that, logically, would have accompanied any movement. I'm not sure which, but someone or something was behind me, not far away.

I slowly turned and saw a dog facing me, perhaps ten meters away, its eyes fixed on my throat, its teeth bared. I could see its pink gums that were spotted with irregular, dark-brown splotches. The dog drooled as it eyed me.

Its brown fur was matted in places with what seemed to be dried blood. One eye drooped and was almost fully closed. Its long tail and its ears pointed to the sky.

As I looked into its one good eye, the dog emitted a low, deep growl that rumbled from the back of its throat. It showed me its yellowed fangs. The dog seemed poised to rush me.

I slowly reached behind my back, under my suit jacket, and gripped my pistol with my right hand. I pulled the weapon out of its holster and, moving as slowly as I could to avoid provoking the animal, I lowered my gun to my right side, ready, if necessary, to raise my arm and fire at the animal.

The dog seemed to sense my intent, and growled louder, its teeth now seeming to grow larger as it took a cautious step toward me.

Without taking my eyes from the animal or moving my weapon, I slipped my left hand into my jacket's side pocket and scooped up a handful of loose watermelon seeds. I slowly withdrew my hand, kneeled, and offered the dog my left hand, palm up and open, full of seeds.

The animal hesitated, then took several tentative steps toward me. Its good eye never left my eyes. It no longer growled.

I nodded and said, using a gentle voice, and speaking to the animal using the Shanghainese *Hu* dialect of the streets I'd been raised to speak, hoping that the dog, too, had been raised to understand some phrases of this vernacular dialect, "*Ayeeyah - Heh!* Come on, wild dog. Come on, boy. No one's going to hurt you."

I continued to nod my head several times as I spoke softly. I reached out my left hand, closer to the animal.

The dog cautiously eased its way over to me and sniffed my palm as it continued to watch me. It took some watermelon seeds into its mouth, chewed and swallowed them, then lapped up another mouthful when it finished the first batch. It never took its good eye from my eyes as it accepted my offering.

When my hand was empty, I slowly reached into my left pocket again, refilled my palm, and offered a second handful of seeds to the animal.

The dog again consumed my entire offering. When it finished and I made no move to again refill my palm, it eventually turned away from me and trotted back into some deep part of the stand of trees where I no longer could see it

I relaxed again and turned my attention back to the Baby Wall.

My father was Chinese, my mother, British. The Chinese refer to me as *low faan* — a barbarian — because I am not full-blooded Chinese. The British refer to me as *mongrel* — a half-breed — because I am part Chinese, not full-blooded Caucasian British.

As far as I'm concerned, I *am* Chinese, a Celestial Being of the Middle Kingdom, by birth, by appearance, by culture, and by temperament. I also am, by disposition and familial training, a Confucian, taught to believe in rules and in order, but also taught to be practical. I like to think I am a healthy blend of modern eastern Oriental exoticism and western Occidental pragmatism.

As I occasionally do on my nights off, or in the evenings after I've completed my day's duty, I am keeping vigil near the Baby Wall. Specifically, I am watching its Baby Drawer to catch any parents who might be disposed to make a deposit into the drawer.

The Baby Wall is across the street from the Race Course in the International Settlement. The Baby Drawer, which is set into the ten-foot-high brick Baby Wall, consists of a small, wooden facing-panel painted with Chinese characters that roughly translate into English as, *Place the baby here.*

The wall, with its drawer, stands outside the western boundary of Saint Mark's Church — an American missionary church — and operates like the night-deposit drawer found outside the Hong Kong & Shanghai Bank building at No. 12, the Bund, except that the deposits made into the Baby Drawer are newborn infants wrapped in dirty cotton blankets, not currency or gold or silver specie.

Tonight, as on all the other nights when I've watched the Baby Drawer, I have come here to rescue male newborns abandoned by their parents — turning the infants over to the Chinese Benevolent Society for care when I find them alive — and to arrest the parents who abandon their male newborns when I catch them in the act of forsaking their children to the fate of the cold in winter or the heat in summer.

As for female babies, I also turn them over for care when I find any alive, and I notify the morgue when I find an infant female corpse. I do not, however, arrest the parents of female infants left in the Baby Drawer unless I see signs that the child was murdered. After all, people in China, including in

Shanghai, have sold or given away their daughters every day since the beginning of time. Leaving their girl children in the Baby Drawer seems to me to be a distinction without a difference.

CHAPTER 2

TALL, SLIM, TWENTY-THREE-YEAR-OLD ALINKA NOVIKOSHA, a White Russian woman with a face that was at once both sad and hungry — a face that knew much, but revealed little — ran her fingers through her short, coal-black hair as she stepped out onto the sidewalk along Nanking Road, and strode away from the entrance of the *Wing On* department store, the International Settlement's most modern and largest shopping emporium.

As she crossed the sidewalk, heading toward the curb to hail a taxi, she could hear the rattling coughs of automobile engines running along the muddy street, their wheels sloshing in the filthy detritus that accumulated each day before the street cleaners came at night to perform their never-ending effort to remove that day's filth.

Alinka paused a few feet from the curb and looked around for a Silver Line taxicab to carry her home from the Settlement to her tree-lined street — Avenue Joffre — in Shanghai's treaty-area popularly known as Frenchtown, but officially called the French Concession.

She was immediately accosted by a skinny, elderly man dressed in a pair of threadbare, khaki shorts, a dirty, torn tee-shirt, and a crushed, torn derby hat missing part of its brim.

The man stepped directly in front of Alinka and, placing his unwashed, malodorous face just inches from hers, screeched, "*Wang ba-tso, Missy? – Rickshaw, Miss? Where you go?*"

Alinka shook her head. *That's just what I need,* she thought, *a reckless, dangerous, jarring ride home that will cover me with mud and filth thrown up from the streets as we bounce along.* She shook her head at the rickshaw coolie, looked away, then quickly stepped around him.

Not seeing a cab waiting along the curb — an unusual occurrence along Nanking Road, the Settlement's principle retail shopping street — she gripped the ribbon tied around the package she cradled in her arm and, now swinging the package as she walked with a decidedly Western bounce in her step, headed toward the Bund where she would board the electric streetcar to take her home.

As she walked, she thought about the over-priced hat she'd just purchased. She knew she would wear it, based on her past practice, only two or three times, then give it to her elderly *Amah* — her elderly head-servant — to bestow on one of the flower-seller girls who worked in her sporting house.

In this way, using this indirect method to select the hat's recipient, Alinka would maintain distance between herself and her employees. At the same time, she also would emphasize her *Amah's* status since the old woman would be the one who selected the woman who would receive Alinka's largesse.

Alinka had not always enjoyed the luxury of dealing with expensive purchases with such frivolity. That certainly had not been the case when she and her parents arrived in Shanghai in 1919, when, as a seven-year-old, she and her parents had fled the Bolsheviks, traveling without money or possessions from Moscow to Vladivostok in Russia, then on to Harbin in Manchuria, and finally settling in Shanghai, a city where anyone could enter and live, whether or not they had a passport, a visa, or work papers, none of which Alinka or her parents had carried with them once they'd been made stateless by the Bolsheviks.

But that was ancient, although not forgotten, history for Alinka. Since that time, her parents had died, and Alinka had clawed her way up to a lofty, professional position, but then had precipitously fallen from that perch. Now, once again, she was resolutely crawling her way back up to near the top, although, by custom and commercial preferences, she never again would be able to regain her former, eminent stature.

Alinka's trip today to the *Wing On* department store was the weekly balm she used to lessen the emotional pain she continued to feel from her precipitous drop in status at age eighteen. *Wing On*, her weekly escape into fantasy, was a decidedly modern department store catering to Oriental as well as Occidental tastes. You could find anything there — American cameras, clothing, perfumes, whiskey, and shoes. Also, Italian leather, Swiss watches, British fountain pens, and Swiss or Italian chocolates. There also were Chinese herbs, silk, satin and other materials, medicines, and art, all on the fifth floor, a gambling den on the third floor, and female comfort for rent on the fourth floor. And even more. Pretty much whatever a customer might want, provided the customer could pay the asking price. All under one roof.

Alinka's shopping routine was simple and always the same. She would arrive at *Wing On* — usually on Monday — and have her hair trimmed and styled in the latest Western short-bob fashion copied from the American films that so pleased

Alinka and her clients. Then she would shop for a few hours, usually buying one over-priced item she knew she would enjoy a few times before giving it away, — today a hat, other days a dress or shoes or a piece of jewelry — and then would finish her restorative excursion at *Wing On* by meeting with Louis Gateaux, the store's sole Frenchman.

For the next ninety minutes, Alinka would submit herself to Monsieur Gateaux, the magician who performed miracles with his hands and with his makeup as he kneaded and then painted the harsh scar that snaked from just below Alinka's right ear, down across her right cheek, ending its crawl under the tip of her chin.

Each week at *Wing On*, in return for a steep off-the-books fee and for occasional sexual favors he demanded — favors that Alinka willingly provided — Monsieur Gateaux softened the damaged skin with his strong, massaging hands, and camouflaged the scar, using his expensive, miracle makeup products.

When Alinka followed the Frenchman's instructions — which she usually did — and avoided washing the part of her face that showcased the scar, Monsieur Gateaux's restorative treatment could last for six or seven days before it had to be renewed.

CHAPTER 3

I THOUGHT ABOUT THE BABY DRAWER as I stood in the thicket waiting for parents to arrive.

Sometimes the newborns were alive when left there, but then died if not found in time to rescue them. Occasionally the infants had already died before they were abandoned, although this was unusual since most dead newborns were left in fields and alleys, or were fed to the Whangpoo River, not placed in a drawer created by foreign missionaries.

I made it my business, my unpleasant but necessary duty, to lurk in sight of the Baby Wall at least one night each week, because nabbing people who offended the peace was my business as a police officer. Parents who deposited their male babies into these drawers offended my sense of order and also violated our municipal laws.

⁕

I hunched my shoulders as I waited. I pulled my coat collar tightly closed to fend off the chilly wind and to block the light snow that had started falling. I reached into my side coat pocket and grabbed the few watermelon seeds that remained from among all those I had given to the dog. As was my habit, I chewed the seeds to occupy my mind while I watched over the Baby Drawer.

After a few minutes passed, I again heard the dog behind me. I immediately regretted I had eaten the few left-over seeds. I slowly reached behind my back to grip my pistol and, in the same motion, slowly turned to face the dog.

The animal stood about seven meters away, facing me. This time its ears and tail pointed down, just the opposite of last time, suggestion submission rather than dominance or aggression, as before. Its mouth was open, as if it was panting from running, but its teeth were not bared as a threat or warning to me. This time I noticed that its left rear leg was crooked and did not touch the ground, something I hadn't seen before. The leg looked as if it had been broken at some time, but had not healed properly.

The dog stared at me.

I released the grip on my pistol, kneeled down, and patted my thigh. "Come here, little dog," I said, again speaking *Hu* to it. "Come here."

The dog stiffened at first, then relaxed.

"It's okay, wild dog, you can come here. I won't hurt you," I said softly.

I patted my thigh again and avoided looking directly into the dog's one good eye. I also avoided smiling so I would not seem to be threatening it by baring my teeth.

The animal took two tentative steps toward me, then hesitated. If it decided to attack me, I would not be able to straighten up and pull out my weapon to shoot it in time to defend myself. My kneeling position certainly gave the wild dog an advantage over me.

I patted my leg again and made a kissing sound with my lips.

The dog limped over to me. I stroked its head, then lightly patted its back.

"Good dog," I said, as I lightly rubbed its back. "Good wild dog."

The dog and I pursued this ritual off and on while I resumed my watch over the Baby Wall. After a while, it settled on the cold ground by my feet. Before it laid down, however, I peeked under its body to determine if I was dealing with a male dog or with a bitch. The dog was female.

After another thirty minutes passed, I saw a small woman slowly approach the Baby Wall. She carried a tiny bundle under her arm that could have been a loaf of bread were it not wrapped in a blanket. She stopped in front of the wall, looked at the closed drawer directly in front of her, then tentatively opened it. She immediately slammed the drawer closed with an attention-grabbing clang.

She repeated this process twice more before finally taking the bundle from under her arm and carefully placing it into the drawer. She uttered some words I couldn't make out as she closed the drawer, then turned to shuffle away.

I kept my hand on the woman's shoulder, gently enough not to frighten her, but firmly enough to arrest her attention.

"Is that your infant, Auntie," I said, "the baby you just deposited into the Baby Drawer?"

She looked up at me with terror in her eyes. I realized she probably was younger than my thirty-six years, maybe was twenty-five or twenty-six years old, but looked to me as if she was in her well-worn fifties.

I made a quick survey of her other physical features. She was thin and short — maybe 1.75 meters tall at the most — and poorly dressed. Her hair was dark, as were her eyes, like the eyes of all Chinese women in Shanghai.

I knew she was not a Sampan-boat woman because, if she had been, she would have disposed of the baby over the side of the boat into the Whangpoo River or into Soochow Creek. She would not have taken the trouble to bring the infant to the Baby Wall, would not have suffered the risk of arrest involved in doing so.

She was terrified as she looked up at me, shaking as if she were palsied.

I pulled out my warrant card ID and flashed it at her, although I doubted she could read it. And, even if she could have read it, I didn't think she would have felt any better knowing I was an SMP Special Branch inspector detective rather than a common mugger.

"*Ayeeyah — Hold on!* I'm a policeman, Auntie," I said, speaking *Hu* to her, explaining why I'd had the audacity to stop her.

She said, "*Quing — Please.* I not do anything wrong. I go now." She glanced down at the ground before looking back up at me.

I nodded that I understood her, but then shook my head to indicate that I knew better than to believe her. I said, "Let's look in that drawer, Auntie," as I tilted my head toward the depository drawer she'd just stepped away from.

"*Bó! — No!*" she squealed, covering her mouth with her gnarled hand.

I looked hard at her, took her elbow, and eased her toward

the Baby Wall. "Be quiet," I said. Then I pulled the drawer open.

The Baby Drawer held a tiny object wrapped in a filthy, dark-blue blanket. I turned and briefly looked at the woman who was staring at me.

"Don't move," I said, then turned back and removed the bundle from the drawer. I carefully placed it on the snow-covered ground.

There was no movement from the blanket. I unwrapped it just enough to see the child, to see that it was lifeless, its sallow skin slightly blue and mottled as death worked it processes.

I unwrapped the bundle just enough to see the baby's sex. The child was a male. I didn't unwrap the blanket any further to see if the infant had any bruises on its body. There were none I could see where the baby was exposed. The morgue would determine if the baby had been beaten to death or strangled, a not uncommon occurrence among Shanghai's destitute coolie class.

"Not mine," the woman said, also speaking in the *Hu* dialect. Her voice was soft, but quivering with fear. "Found boy baby in street. Put in drawer for keeping safe." She stared at me with pleading eyes.

I considered her tacit, but obvious request.

I could honor her silent plea, let her go, and chalk this crime up to the natural by-product of the woman's coolie-class, abject, life circumstances, then have the baby's body picked up and disposed of by a morgue attendant, without making an arrest. Or, I could arrest the woman, since the baby was male, and let the magistrate deal with her after I brought her in.

I considered both options.

Then I arrested her.

We walked back to the station house. The woman walked in front, with me giving her prodding, verbal directions from time-to-time. I carried the infant's wrapped corpse under my left arm, like a loaf of freshly baked bread from Frenchtown, much as the woman had carried the bundle when she approached the Baby Wall. The dog slowly limped alongside me, never straying far from my right leg.

I bent over several times as we walked and patted the dog's head or its back. It seemed not to mind.

I decided I would keep the dog at home as a pet until it decided to run off, as it surely would some time since it was a wild dog. Until then, because of its sex, I decided to call it *Bik — Jade* — the adopted Chinese name of my deceased British mother.

CHAPTER 4

CHANG SIN GREW UP ON a river-sailing boat. Although he was seven years old, he had never set foot on land.

One week after he passed his seventh birthday — an event unnoticed by the boy or by his family — Sin's father sold him to a stranger who had a house in Fukien Provence.

In return for his son, Sin's father received sufficient silver tael to sustain Sin's remaining family, as well as the Song Dynasty-style river-sailing Junk they lived aboard, for approximately two years, even if Sin's birth family did not earn another single yuan during that time sailing the Whangpoo and other South China rivers selling their scavenged wares.

Sin was not the first boy purchased by the stranger who had acquired him. This man also had purchased a young boy, who was eight years old when Sin was purchased, who he treated as a son, and who he trained in the *Shaolin* and *Wing Chun* Forms of martial arts, two Forms the man excelled at and, when he still was a young man many decades ago, had taught to others.

"If you are obedient, my youngest son," the man said to Sin that first day, "and if you learn your lessons well, you will be safe here, well-fed, well cared for, and reasonably happy.

"If you disobey me or if you do not master your training, you will be punished and, perhaps, will die by my hand."

Sin, shivering with fear as only a seven-year-old child could who was under the control of a stranger, said nothing.

"Did you hear what I said?" the man asked, deliberately speaking softly.

"Yes, sir," Sin said. He stared at the courtyard soil before his feet.

The man frowned. "My name is not *sir*, young boy. You will call me, *Master*."

"Yes, Master."

They were standing in the front courtyard of a three-story structure, located in Amoy, that would be Sin's new home. Walls — twelve-feet high and topped with barbed wire — surrounded the structure and its bare yard on all sides.

The ground under Sin's feet felt as strange to him, since he was used to the rolling motion of his family's Junk, as the deck of a river-going ship would have felt at first to a person who had never been to sea. He did not easily adjust to the stillness of the Earth beneath his feet, shifting his weight from leg to leg as if he expected the ground beneath him to suddenly undulate.

"Wait here, Chang Sin," the master said, as he turned away from him, leaving Sin standing alone in the courtyard.

The master soon returned, followed by his other son.

The boy was a full head taller than Sin, and a quarter of Sin's weight heavier. He readily exhibited, as he walked out into the courtyard and eyed Sin for the first time, the maturity given him by the one-year age advantage he had over seven-year-old Sin.

"This is your new brother, Sin," the master said, tilting his head toward the eight-year-old. "His name is Gan Hao. Until the day you are required to fight one another to the death, you will act as brothers in all regards."

"Yes, Master," Sin said.

"Come now, Sin and Hao. Sit at my feet like obedient sons while I tell you what your lives will be like, and the missions you will strive to achieve for me, beginning tomorrow.

CHAPTER 5

BIG-EARED TU, AS TU YU KUNG was known throughout China and the Occidental world, sat at a table with his former boss, Huang Jinrong, the man commonly known as Pock-Marked Huang.

Huang had once been the undisputed leader of the Green Dragon Society, an organization commonly known as the Green Gang, a criminal triad having such illustrious and influential members as the revolutionary leader and first president of the Republic, Sun Yat-sen, and the current head of the Republic's Kuomintang government and military, Chiang Kai-shek.

Pock-Marked Huang had been the person who, in 1926, had invited Big-Eared Tu to join the criminal triad, only to wake up one day two years later to find that Tu had pushed him aside and now headed the criminal enterprise. Tu had become Pock-Marked Huang's boss.

Big-Eared Tu reached into a pocket hidden deep in the folds of his long, mint-color Mandarin gown, and extracted a pack of *Three Cats* brand cigarettes.

He reached across the table and offered a smoke to Huang. When Huang hesitated, Tu said, "Take it."

Tu was not being polite. He was asserting his authority over Huang, as he felt required to do from time-to-time, to remind Huang that he now worked for and answered to Tu.

Tu — in terms of his Confucian traditional outward dress and public bearing, his insincere yet generous charitable endeavors, and his misdirecting, smiling disposition — presented to all the world all the indicia of a prominent, upstanding, and law-abiding citizen living in a major urban area.

In 1933, Shanghai's version of *Who's Who* published an entry for Big-Eared Tu which indicated that he was the president of, or sat on the boards of directors of, four banks, three hospitals, seven prominent charities, the Shanghai General Chamber of Commerce, the French Concession's Chamber of Commerce, two expensive private schools, the Cotton Exchange, and the Chinese Merchant Steam Navigation Company, China's most important commercial sailing line.

What *Who's Who* did not state was that Big-Eared Tu also was the leader of the largest criminal triad in China and operating in the United States. In this capacity, he controlled the extensive opium trade in Shanghai, most gambling in the city, had a financial piece of the extensive Flowery Kingdom industry, received payoffs from all nightclubs, cabarets, and theaters, and received payoffs from all hotels and apartment buildings.

Who's Who also failed to mention that Tu operated an extensive protection service which specialized in extorting money from small merchants, and that he had in his pocket most members of the three Shanghai municipal police forces, including the one headed by Pock-Marked Huang, who Tu had arranged to become the chief-of-police in Frenchtown.

Who's Who also did not indicate that Tu (through his common membership with him in the Green Gang) had formed a close alliance with Chiang Kai-shek to drive Mao Tse-tung and his Communist Party forces out of Shanghai. In return, Chiang, who publicly professed to oppose the sale and use of opium, turned a blind eye to Tu's ever-growing opium empire, although he did exact a stiff tax on all opium sold in the city. This tax supplied Chiang's Kuomintang Party with a steady stream of much needed revenue for its use against the Communists and for general graft.

After Huang took a cigarette from him, Tu retrieved his own from the *Three Cats* pack, put it into the corner of his mouth, and waited while Huang stood up, walked around the table, and lit the cigarette for him.

When Huang had returned to his seat, Tu said, "You are sure that Zhing-ru has stolen from us?" Tu spoke Mandarin.

"He is the one," Huang said, replying in Shanghainese.

Tu drew deeply on his cigarette, briefly held the smoke in his lungs, then forcibly blew out the smoke, intentionally streaming it across the table directly onto Huang.

"No doubt about this?" he asked.

"No, Master Tu. No doubt."

Tu stabbed his cigarette out on the table top.

"Have Zhing-ru's children strangled in front of him and his wife. Then have his wife raped five or six times by your men while Zhing-ru watches. When that is complete, have Zhing-ru strangled in front of his wife."

He paused a beat.

"After that, give the woman to a coolie-whore house on the waterfront. Make it clear we will not want her back when she has been used up and is no longer earning her keep."

CHAPTER 6

I LOVE BEING A POLICEMAN IN Shanghai. More specifically, I love being an inspector detective here because I love this pleasure-mad, rapacious, corrupt, over-crowded, noisy, strife-ridden, licentious, opulent, seedy, and decadent city of contrasts.

I have lived all my life in Chapei — the walled-city section of the old Chinese city in the International Settlement. This part of the Settlement is commonly known as the Old City. It was the part of Shanghai where the invading Japanese army fought our Nineteenth Route Army in 1932, in what became known as the January 28 Incident.

Growing up, I lived just one-half a street from the railway station with my mother, father, and my six siblings, including my eldest brother, called Ling Sun-Yu.

I'd never left Chapei, and had never seen the rest of Shanghai, until I was fourteen years old. That was when my late father, a carpenter by trade, took me with him one day to Frenchtown. He wanted me to help him with a small construction job he would perform there.

Once I saw the French Concession, with its wide, tree-lined streets, opulent homes, and tall buildings, I vowed that someday I would find my way out of the Chinese Old City, and would never return there to live. It took me eight more years before I was able to move away from Chapei, but when that time came, I chose to stay where I was. I continue to live in Chapei to this day.

When I was sixteen years old, and Eldest Brother was twenty-one, our parents, encouraged by the Lutheran missionaries who had converted my father from Taoism to Protestantism, sent us to San Francisco in America to study for four years at the mission college run by the Lutheran Church. Eldest Brother and I entered the school at the same time and in the same grade even though we were five years apart in age. Fortunately, for most of our lives, our British mother had spoken English, as well as Mandarin Chinese, to us, and had insisted that we learn to read both languages. As a result, Eldest Brother and I were able to pass our university courses and exams without difficulty.

School was free for us, including our food and a place to live, all paid for by the Lutheran Church. The only catch was that our parents had agreed that when Eldest Brother and I graduated college, we would return to Shanghai and become missionaries for the church.

When we returned to Shanghai after completing our studies, neither Eldest Brother nor I honored that pledge. We didn't feel bad about this since we hadn't been the ones to make it in the first place, and likely, if asked to make it at the time, would not have agreed to do so.

After returning home from America, I took a job working in the International Settlement (where the British and Americans mostly lived and worked). I was employed as an entry-level foot-patrol constable with the SMP. I was fortunate that my parents had insisted that Eldest Brother and I complete our education. Otherwise, I would not have passed the entrance exam required to join the police.

I was sitting at my desk in the municipal police station thinking about this when someone cleared his throat. I looked up, feigning surprise, although I knew from the tone of the sound who I would find standing in front of me when I looked up.

"*Ayeeyah — Hello*, Most Honorable Chief Inspector," I said, as I quickly stood up and slightly bowed my head to demonstrate the respect demanded by his position with the SMP.

"Sit," the chief inspector said, motioning me back to my chair with the sweep of his hand.

I sat back down and waited to find out why Chief Inspector Chapman — my boss — had come to my desk, rather than summon me to his office as he typically did when he wanted to see me. I couldn't remember this ever happening before. It made me uneasy.

"I say, Sun-jin, Old Man, I have permitted the coolie woman you arrested to leave." He looked directly into my eyes. "You know you had no business arresting her."

Even though the Baby Wall lady was only one of several coolie women I'd arrested last evening and this morning for various offenses, I knew he was referring to the woman from the Baby Wall.

"But—" I said.

"No *but*, Sun-jin," he said. "You act as if you are new to this position, a constable still trying to make his name, but you are not, and you know better."

"But—" I said again.

"Tell me this, Inspector Detective," Chief Inspector Chapman said to me, "was there any sign of foul play on the baby's body?"

I shook my head.

"Did the coroner say there was foul play?"

"No."

"Did the woman assault you when you arrested her?"

"You know she didn't, sir. It would have been in my report."

"Then take pity on her," he said. "You don't know how many mouths she has to feed, what her life is like. This child might have been one child too many, the one she had to dispose of to save herself and the rest of her family."

"Maybe," I said, but thinking, *You don't know that either, yet you set her free.*

"Or perhaps the infant died from natural causes and the woman could not afford to bury him with a proper funeral," he said, "and hoped the missionaries would do so for her."

"The point is, Sun-jin, you are being too rigid in dealing with this and other local matters. Life isn't as clear cut as you would like to see it. It's time you realized that."

I said nothing.

"You need to accept that the Baby Drawer is a fact of life in Shanghai. It was here before us and it will be here long after we're gone.

"Remind yourself, Old Chap, whenever you waiver, that the Baby Drawer is preferable to having an infant left in a vacant lot, dead or alive, a target for wandering dogs to tear apart and devour."

The chief inspector and I have had this discussion, in many different contexts, many times before, always with the same result, always with the chief inspector warning me that I have to start seeing the gray areas of life if I want to successfully continue as a SMP inspector detective. As always, I promised to try harder. As always, the chief inspector rolled his eyes.

"Complete your paperwork for this," he said, "but do not mention the woman. State only that you found the baby in the drawer and that it was dead when you found it, with the person who placed it there unknown."

"Yes, Chief Inspector," I said.

I was stubborn, but not foolish. I had my orders and I cherished my job, so I would fall into line on this issue — until next time.

CHAPTER 7

T HE DAY THE MASTER INTRODUCED Sin and Hao to one another, he instructed them to meet him in the courtyard that morning at 4:00 a.m. They were told to appear there bare-chested and barefoot, and not to be even one minute late.

"*Ayeeyah*! — *May the Gods be mournful!*" the master said, shaking his head as he looked from Hao to Sin under the light of the quarter moon. "You are a sorry, soft-looking pair. Well, that will soon change."

The master explained to Sin that he would instruct him in two Forms of martial arts — *Shaolin and Wing Chun* — just as he'd already started instructing Hao many months before.

"You will train and study the Forms as if your life depends on your skill — as it will. You will become a master of the Forms, qualified to teach others, as I shall teach you.

"One day, when I so instruct you," he said, looking first at Sin and then at Hao, "you will challenge one another. Only one of you will survive. The other we will together feed to the dogs. The survivor will become my weapon. My assassin for hire."

CHAPTER 8

THERE HAS NEVER BEEN ANY love lost between Eldest Brother — as Confucian custom requires I refer to and directly address Sun-yu — and me. And this has had nothing to do with the difference in our ages. It has had everything to do with our respective world views and values.

Because I am a cop (or, maybe, I am a cop because this is the way I see the world), I have always lived by rules, and have venerated the order that rules offer. That was the Confucian influence I — but for some reason, not Eldest Brother — absorbed from our departed, blessed father.

Sun-yu sees rules as starting points. I see them as a self-contained end points. That outlook on life, more than anything else, explains our fundamental conflict in a way no long texts of Confucian or Taoist philosophy could ever better explain. It also states the continuing difference that lives on between us.

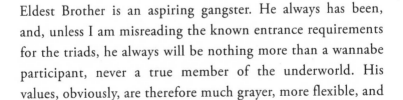

Eldest Brother is an aspiring gangster. He always has been, and, unless I am misreading the known entrance requirements for the triads, he always will be nothing more than a wannabe participant, never a true member of the underworld. His values, obviously, are therefore much grayer, more flexible, and definitely more pragmatic than mine. That probably explains why Eldest Brother is a Taoist, not a Confucian.

One of the continuing problems that exists between Eldest Brother and me has been that I continually fail to show him the proper familial respect due to the eldest brother of a family. This most frequently has become an issue between us when, over the years, Eldest Brother has ordered me to give up my job as a policeman and to come to work for him. I have always refused to do anything so foolish, of course. I think Sun-yu has never forgiven me for having disobeyed him in this regard.

This continuing problem between us demonstrates the irony of our relative positions and how strange that is. For example, I, as a Confucian who loves rules and who strives to obey rules, for the most part, should always adhere to and strictly practice the dogma of family and sibling fealty, showing due respect for Sun-yu, as my eldest brother. For example, I should follow his instruction to me to leave my policeman's job and come to work for him. But I don't.

And, to show the other side of our problem, Sun-yu, as a devout Taoist and pragmatist who deals in a world of gray reality, shouldn't care that I usually do not show him proper Confucian deference. Yet he cares greatly.

Eldest Brother, for many years now, has owned a nightclub called the Heavenly Palace. The club is located on Avenue Edouard VII in the French Concession.

The club has been the perfect vehicle for Sun-yu's varied, but unrealized, criminal ambitions. It has brought him steady cash flow and good *joss* — good *luck*. It has permitted him to play the role of generous host and showman to Shanghai's underworld, a role he cherishes because it feeds his ego and fits in with his fantasy that he is a successful criminal, associating with others of like mind and desires.

When Sun-yu purchased the Heavenly Palace eight years ago — it then was named the Pale Tea Club — he immediately changed its name, upgraded its interior décor to western-style Art deco, and eliminated several of the policies imposed by its former owner — policies which restricted the club's clientele to white Occidentals only — arbitrary practices that were then driving the business toward bankruptcy.

Eldest Brother changed all that. Under Sun-yu's ownership and management, the only color the club recognizes is the color of gold, silver, and folding money. All cultures and races — white, Chinese, Jewish, Slavic, Colored, Russian, and Japanese, among others — are welcome if they can pay their way. In addition, Sun-yu offers free drinks to women guests who are under twenty years of age, and to members of Shanghai's criminal triads of every age. As a result of these measures, business at the Heavenly Palace has boomed ever since Eldest Brother took over ownership of the club.

One of Eldest Brother's first new practices when he assumed ownership of his club has proven to be very popular. For the club's entertainment, Eldest Brother has brought in a different American jazz quartet or jazz band every two weeks, American jazz having been a favorite style of music in Shanghai since the late 1920s. My favorite group was last month's band — *Buck Clayton & his Harlem Gentleman* — who somehow Eldest Brother persuaded to quit their lucrative contract at the Canidrome Ballroom, and to appear instead at his second-rate club in Frenchtown. This achievement made me wonder: Maybe Eldest Brother had become an accomplished gangster after all, and I just didn't see it. How else could he persuade the Buck Clayton band to break its contract at one of the most famous nightclubs in Shanghai, and come join him instead?

The club's other popular entertainment is taxi dancing — purchasing a ticket to pay the cost of dancing with a hostess. Eldest Brother operates this form of entertainment on the second floor of the club, once again ignoring Shanghai customs by permitting both Chinese and White Russian women to act as taxi dancers and as flower-seller girls, all having access to rooms to rent by the hour on the fourth floor of the club.

Although Eldest Brother does not care about the various races or cultures of his taxi-dancing hostesses, he does care very much how attractive and how enticing his taxi dancers look. Eldest Brother's taxi-dancing hostesses are all tall, slim, and beautiful. Otherwise, Eldest Brother doesn't hire them.

Eldest Brother's taxi-dancing hostesses all wear fashionable, tight-fitting dresses — called *chi-pao* — which cling to their bodies and are slit on the right side from their ankle-length hems up to the middle of the women's hips. Sun-yu's taxi-dancing hostesses, as do hostesses in most of the other clubs, wear these seductive dresses with tall high-heels.

As is the custom in most nightclubs, the taxi-dancing hostesses sit together on folding chairs and wait for the customers — men and women — to approach them, each hoping the next customer will choose her. Those women anxious to dance indicate this by sitting in the front two rows of chairs. Those who are tired and want time off, by custom, sit in the back two rows with their shoes removed.

Sun-yu's hostesses dance for tickets. The women charge from 10¢ to $1.00, Shanghai silver, per dance, depending on the women's ages, with the older women charging far less per dance than the younger hostesses charge.

The club requires that the customers, in addition to buying tickets to dance, also buy bottles of champagne that are to be emptied between dances with the help of the hostesses. The champagne is a coarse, cheap variety and is grossly overpriced. Most customers, knowing this, do not seem to mind. They are not present on the second floor of the Heavenly Palace to drink champagne.

The hostesses receive a percentage of the cost of each customer's dance ticket, which the hostesses redeems at the end of the night, and a share of money accumulated from the drinks purchased by their customers. An energetic taxi dancer at Eldest Brother's club, if she chooses to, can make a good living without ever participating in the flower-seller girl aspect of the job that is common in most clubs, including the Heavenly Palace.

The club is very popular with all races and cultures, but especially favored among young male Chinese gangsters, who otherwise rarely have the opportunity to rub elbows with, and to strut their egos and cash before, Occidentals.

These ambitious young Chinese men enjoy wearing Western-style clothing, having their hair cut in the latest Western styles, and having their hair groomed with Brilliantine. This group includes young members of the Green Gang, who frequent the club, and who, by their presence, offer Eldest Brother the imagined opportunity to share in their power merely by reason of his proximity to them.

I respect Sun-yu for his achievement in having taken a dying nightclub and making it popular and profitable. But I also know that as the club becomes more and more successful, one day he will forcibly lose the club to the Green Gang. That is the way of Shanghai.

CHAPTER 9

I WAS SITTING AT MY DESK, working my way through reports, and adding materials to the detailed files I keep on current cases I am working, as well as on suspended cases I have unsuccessfully worked, when a call came in to the front desk from the House of Multiple Joys. The caller said that the body of a young woman — a flower-seller girl employed by the sporting house — had been found by the coolie maid in the girl's entertaining room shortly before the call. Chief Inspector Chapman assigned the case to me.

Normally such calls do not receive priority attention since the murder of a flower-seller girl — other than those at the exalted courtesan level — is considered an expected by-product of the life these women have chosen for themselves, a hazard of doing business. But it is well known among the police that the House of Multiple Joys is not the usual Flowery Kingdom sporting house. The House of Multiple Joys is an up-scale operation, known in the trade as a Number Three house, that occasionally is visited by such luminaries as famed Shanghai architects George Leopold Wilson and Brenan Atkinson, by crime bosses Big-Eared Tu and his Frenchtown Police Chief, Pock-Marked Huang, by the real estate moguls Tug Wilson and Victor Sassoon, and by several members of the International Settlement's ruling Municipal Council. Other similarly important people, including high-ranking officers in the Settlement's SMP and its Special Branch, where I work, also are known to use the services from time-to-time of the House of Multiple Joys.

"Sun-jin, Old Man," Chief Inspector Chapman said, "you will observe protocol and be discreet when you investigate this unfortunate incident. You will remember that this event indirectly touches on the lives of some very important citizens and city rulers."

"I understand," I said, nodding. I slightly bowed my head.

"Dispose of this matter, including the body of the flower-seller girl, as quickly and quietly as you can," the chief inspector added.

I understood. I would investigate the crime with only a superficial nod toward solving it. Then everyone would be happy except for the unfortunate, disposable woman who no longer had her job at the House of Multiple Joys.

Shanghai's principle upscale sporting house area — a section of the city known as the Line — is found along Kiangse Road, perpendicular to the Bund, and parallel to Nanking Road. The Line is populated by licensed gambling houses, by a few licensed opium dens, by several licensed upscale, Number Three sporting houses, and by many unlicensed, illegal, middle-level brothels along the area commonly known as Blood Alley.

Some of the most beautiful and accomplished flower-seller girls in Shanghai work in the Number Three, upscale houses. They cater to all manner of sexual tastes and to most levels of available disposable yuan or Shanghai silver dollars.

Only a few of these houses offer the customer a choice of girls of different races. If a customer wants a Chinese woman, the customer generally visits one of several houses populated by Oriental women. These women mainly come from Soochow because the women from Soochow are believed to be the most beautiful women in China and to be the best trained in the pillow arts.

If the customer wants an Occidental woman, he visits a brothel that offers either American women or White Russian women. Both these groups of flower-seller girls also are very beautiful or they are not hired by the sporting houses. They also are known to be very accommodating. The House of Multiple Joys is staffed with American women.

I had awakened early in the morning before the call came in to the station house from the House of Multiple Joys. As I usually do, I started my day at home by practicing the ancient Chinese martial art known as *Shaolin*. I have been studying this Form since I was thirteen years old, and have continued to practice it, although without the aid of a master-teacher to instruct me. This is because my job as an SMP Special Branch policeman — both as a constable, at first, and now as an inspector detective — has made my working hours so irregular I cannot control my practice schedule. The best I can do now is practice by myself (developing, I'm sure, bad habits along the way) every morning.

I joined the International Settlement's SMP, an organization run by the British, two days after my twenty-first birthday. I served as a foot-patrol constable until four years ago when I turned thirty-two and was promoted to the rank of sub-inspector detective. As a constable, and later as a sub-inspector detective, I was assigned to the Central Police Station at 239 Hankow Road. When I finally was promoted to inspector detective, I moved to the station house located along the eastern boundary of the Settlement, contiguous to the French Concession, at 2049 Pingliang Road. That's where I work from now.

I have had a fairly good career as a policeman. In 1930, while still a constable, I received the Police Distinguished Conduct Medal, Class II, for ". . . great bravery and initiative displayed in challenging a gang of armed desperadoes on Connaught Road, on the evening of April 26, 1930," according to the official certificate hanging on my office wall. While this award has never earned me an increase in salary, it has shielded me from punishment on those few occasions when Chief Inspector Chapman was angry at me for something I'd done or for something I was supposed to have done, but had not.

The International Settlement's SMP is not the only police force covering Shanghai. Because the western powers created extra-territoriality for some sections of Shanghai when they carved up the city after defeating we Chinese in the Opium War in 1842, several police forces emerged to govern their own territories within Shanghai. This meant that their nationals were subject only to the laws and courts of their home country while they were in Shanghai, not to the laws of China.

In this regard, the British handle the International Settlement, excluding the Hongkew section which is policed by the Japanese. The French police the French Concession. And the Chinese police the balance of Shanghai, including Chapei in the Old City portion of the International Settlement.

There is no overlapping jurisdiction among Shanghai's foreign territories, concessions, and the Old City. Each territory is like its own foreign country within its boundaries.

Until seven months ago, an SMP constable or inspector detective was not permitted to enter the Chinese or French areas (and, likewise, for them, if they wanted to come into the International Settlement) to pursue an investigation or to make an arrest for a crime committed in their own, governed territory. In fact, hostility among the several Shanghai police forces is so rampant that the Chinese police have been known to arrest our constables and inspector detectives who enter the Old City, and in some cases to shoot at our officers, even if we only enter to confer with the Chinese authorities.

As a result of these restrictive, enforced limitations, armed robbers, kidnappers, murderers, and other criminals often base themselves in one of the three territories, but commit their crimes in another, thereby avoiding arrest and punishment.

The only exception among the exclusive jurisdiction of the three territories is in the case of hot pursuit. Under the unwritten, informal rule, any officer may chase a suspect into another territory and arrest the suspect, but the burden of proving hot pursuit falls on the arresting police officer. This often has been resolved while the Chinese authorities hold the International Settlement's police officer or the French Concession's officer at gunpoint or, worse, hold him in jail in Chapei.

This changed seven months ago when the three territories entered into a five-year agreement, called the Police Forces' Compact, to allow the police to investigate and make arrests in each other's territories, provided they are accompanied by a local policeman. The old rule of hot pursuit still applies as an exception to this new rule.

The agreement — or the Compact, as it is known — is being tried out as an experiment. It might end in four more years or it could be extended if it seems to help police work.

Although the French, Chinese, and the Japanese entered into the Compact with the British, none of them welcomed it, and they do not enforce it in most instances.

My experience with the Compact so far is that it has barely relieved the threat of being shot at by the Chinese cops, since the Chinese police force seems to resent the very existence of the underlying agreement the Compact represents.

The police force in the International Settlement is made up of approximately four thousand policemen, consisting of many nationalities: many Englishmen and some colonials; many Americans; many Chinese (such as me); a few White Russians; many Japanese; a few Germans; and, some Sikhs who mostly direct traffic. We Chinese are the largest component of the SMP.

As a result of our large numbers, new non-Chinese constables are required to study the difficult Shanghainese dialect of speaking, including the difficult, base, *Hu* dialect. This is a firm requirement of the *Terms and Conditions of Service Agreement* each recruit signs to join the SMP. The recruits take their Chinese lessons very seriously since they either become fluent in the language within a certain time or they are dismissed from the police force and shipped home.

The SMP is modeled after the police force in London (at

least that's what I've been told since I've never been to England to confirm this). As in London, the International Settlement's constables wear a thin blue uniform in spring and autumn, a heavy dark-blue serge suit in winter, and khaki in summer, including short pants — except we Chinese policemen, as a group, uniformly refuse to wear short pants.

One matter concerning all territorial police forces, a matter sometimes raised by the *North China Daily News* and by the *Shanghai Evening Post* — two of several English-language newspapers sold in Shanghai — is what the newsmen and newswomen, such as the American ex-patriate, Emily Hahn, referred to as police corruption.

As the system works, the average monthly salary of an inspector detective is $300, Shanghai folding money. This is hardly enough to pay your bills, have minimum necessities for day-to-day living, and occasionally allow you to splurge on yourself. Even the seventeen days' holidays we receive each year doesn't help. You can't spend your holiday allotment in a shop or nightclub.

I've read the newspaper articles concerning police corruption with much interest, for obvious reasons, but I don't know what the newspapers mean by that phrase. It seemed to me that all the newspapers have done is to show their ignorance about how the various Shanghai police forces work, overlooking the obvious fact that squeeze, as such payments are called in English — what we Chinese call *hóng bāo* — is customary in Shanghai as a means of keeping police salaries low or modest, and yet give the policemen a decent income.

To me, police corruption really means an officer not

doing his job in return for some favor or money he received specifically to influence him not to do his job. But that's not how the system works.

Like all International Settlement policemen I know (and this is true, too, of the police working in the French Concession, of the Japanese in Hongkew, and the Chinese in the Old City), I receive a discreet, monthly cash payment from several merchants in the Settlement, from most madams on behalf of their sporting houses, from most gambling dens, and occasionally from individuals operating within my beat or my sector of coverage. These payments have always been a part of the police system and do not affect how we act toward whoever pays us — as long as the payments are made.

Hóng bāo is so entrenched and so well-understood by everyone, that when you receive a promotion from constable to sub-inspector detective, for example, the amount of squeeze in the envelope you receive automatically increases without you having to say anything. This is what keeps Shanghai running as smoothly and as honestly as a well-oiled machine.

In the four years I've been an inspector detective, I've investigated many murders, armed robberies, kidnappings, and, since the January 28 Incident in 1932 when the Japanese in Shanghai started flexing their muscles and acting up, even a few espionage cases involving Japanese spies.

But these experiences weren't why I was assigned to the flower-seller girl murder case. I suspect that Chief Inspector Chapman assigned me to the homicide at the House of Multiple Joys, not because I had any special skill or experience as an inspector detective that would be required there, but because I was on good terms with most of the madams in the Settlement, including the House of Multiple Joys' madam, Gracie Gale — a woman with whom I once had a short, off-hours affair — and because I am familiar with many of the flower-seller girls who work the Line, going back to when I was a constable walking that neighborhood as my beat.

I reached into my desk drawer for my pistol and strapped it to the side of my chest, under my jacket. As a member of the Special Branch — formerly called the Criminal Investigation Department — I am authorized to carry a firearm with me at all times without seeking permission in each instance, as other, non-Special Branch SMP members are required to do. It was a policy I found very inconvenient before I became a member of the Special Branch, and one I'm happy I do not have to follow any longer.

My choice of weapon, after having tried many different types of revolvers and pistols, is the .45 Colt M1911A1 pistol. It's a bit weighty so that none of my colleagues carry it, but I am used to its heft, and I appreciate its reliability. It has never jammed on me, although some other Special Branch regular-issue pistols have.

I left the station house to begin my investigation. Because I know Gracie Gale on a personal level, and wanted her to view me on this occasion as a police professional working the crime, not as a former lover and sometimes patron of her sporting house, I stopped at my flat before going to Gracie's to change into my best suit of clothes, to shave again, and to pomade my hair.

Having done that, before I left, I set a bowl of water outside for Bik since I didn't see her anywhere around my apartment building. I assumed she would come home to me at some point today or tonight — or not. She was, after all, still a wild dog.

Then I went to the House of Multiple Joys.

CHAPTER 10

S IN HAD NEVER HAD A friend before Hao.

Until the master purchased him in 1931, Sin had lived all his life on board his family's river-Junk, never once — as was the river-peoples' custom — stepping onto land. He had never even seen another child — other than his siblings — except across the expanse of water when his family was in some river or coastal port.

One week after the master introduced them, the seven-year-old Sin and eight-year-old Hao sat in the courtyard of the master's walled-in house in Amoy in Fukien Province. They shared a loaf of bread.

The master had left that morning for Shanghai. He was not expected back for at least one week. He left the boys in the care of a trusted servant.

"You are a river rat," said Hao.

"Not a rat. A river and coastal child. My family sails the rivers and coast between Canton and Haichow, stopping at different ports. I was part of the crew."

"Like I said, a river rat." Hao smirked, tore off the end of the loaf, then handed the bread to Sin.

Sin didn't know whether or not to be offended by this boy's name calling. But, recognizing that Hao was older and therefore physically larger than he was, and likely was more skilled in martial arts since Sin had practiced the two Forms for only one week, not many months like Hao, he decided to say nothing more on the subject.

Sin tore a piece of bread from the loaf, stuffed the piece into his mouth, and passed what remained of the loaf back to the older boy.

"Where are you from?" Sin asked.

"Nowhere. Over there," Hao said, as he canted his head in a northern direction. "Here, too, and everywhere. Amoy now," he said, as he chewed.

"How long have you been the master's son?"

"For eight full moons longer than you," Hao said. He passed back the bread.

Sin thought about the life he'd left behind on the Junk, about his parents, his older brothers, and his sisters. He mentally shrugged. Life already was better with the master than it ever had been aboard the Junk. Here, in Amoy, he was well fed, slept enough so he was not always tired, and was learning some interesting skills as he practiced the two martial arts Forms the master taught him. He had even become used to walking on land.

"Let's spar Push Hands," Hao said, "so when the master returns, he will be pleased with our *Wing Chun* progress."

The master typically spent as much time — sometimes more — away from his house in Amoy as he spent there supervising and educating his sons. He had many interests to attend to in the Celestial Kingdom, including homes in several provinces to look after. Amoy was only one small part of his life, although an important one.

The master's presence in Amoy was not always essential in terms of bringing along his sons. He expected that when he was absent from Amoy, his boys would diligently attend to their martial arts Forms, practicing every day. He also expected that they would diligently attend to reading and contemplating the meanings to be derived from studying and discussing Confucius's ANALECTS, from Sun Tzu's ART OF WAR, and from Lao Tzu's TAO TE CHING. To be certain this occurred, the master tasked his head servant with spying on the boys and reporting back to him if something untoward occurred.

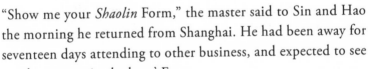

"Show me your *Shaolin* Form," the master said to Sin and Hao the morning he returned from Shanghai. He had been away for seventeen days attending to other business, and expected to see much progress in the boys' Forms.

Sin and Hao stood shoulder to shoulder in front of the master, facing him. They bowed from their waists, then straightened up in unison, turned, and stepped away from the master. They faced one another.

His sons went through the *Shaolin* Form from beginning to end, then turned to spar with one another. They engaged in mock combat for ninety minutes. The master interrupted them from time-to-time to correct a posture or movement, refining their understanding of the classic Form, complementing them when they performed well, chastising them when they were sloppy or inattentive.

At night — on those nights when the master was away from Amoy and the boys were alone, except for the presence of the watchful servant — the boys played card games or rolled dice. Like many Chinese, they enjoyed gambling, and had no problem wagering and risking with one another the small weekly spending allowance they each received from the master. The winner of these games, as a matter of unstated custom, usually paid for the weekly expenses of the other — the loser — until the games' fortunes shifted.

Like many Chinese, the boys also enjoyed watching American films with dubbed-in dialog. At least once each week when the master was away, and sometimes twice to see the same film again, they walked twelve kilometers to the village of Jemei to attend a movie. They particularly enjoyed the Fred Astaire and Ginger Rogers musical films that showed off dance steps that reminded them, in many ways, of their own movements when they practiced the martial arts Forms.

When the master was in Amoy, in the evening after practicing the Forms all day, Sin and Hao would sit by a fire with him. They would diligently attend to their Taoist and Confucian educations, engaging in long, often tedious, boring discussions with the master and with each another.

CHAPTER 11

When Alinka and her parents fled Russia and the advancing Bolshevik army in 1919, life did not improve for them once they reached the safe-haven of Shanghai, although they now were out of danger of being liquidated as enemies of the state.

As was typical of the White Russians while still in Russia, Alinka's family saw their bank account looted by the state, had their passports confiscated, and watched their physical assets and wealth be looted by strangers or confiscated by the state. All Alinka's family were able to bring with them to Shanghai was some cheap jewelry and other small, transportable valuables such as inexpensive, but collectible postage stamps and coins belonging to Alinka's grandfather, a few small religious icons, and some unframed, common paintings that they smuggled out with them.

Shanghai proved to be a mixed blessing for most of the White Russian immigrants. By 1935, there were approximately twenty-five thousand White Russians living in Shanghai, mostly in the French Concession, in a neighborhood locally known as Little Russia.

Because there were so many White Russians settled in Shanghai, their very presence threatened the delicate, mixed-race, and mixed-cultural balance of Shanghai's population. It especially disturbed the British who scorned the White Russian emigrants as undesirable parasites.

The White Russians who fled to Shanghai, for the most part, were middle class merchants, university professors, farmer-peasants, ex-army officers, musicians, middle-school teachers, and artists, although they often claimed, once in Shanghai, to be generals, counts, duchesses, or princesses. They brought with them their skills and their experience in their trades and arts. This proved crucial to their survival in Shanghai.

Very few White Russian men were able to find employment in Shanghai. Many employers, by belief and custom, felt it was undignified for a Caucasian male to work in the service industries, so these employers hired indigenous Chinese who performed the same kind of service work the White Russian males sought, but for far lower wages.

Beyond these custom-based and financial reasons for not hiring White Russian males, by British tradition, office work and retail-sales jobs in department stores were not available to any men in Shanghai unless they either were Eurasian or Portuguese, or unless, in a few instances, they spoke perfect English, the *lingua franca* of mercantile Shanghai. Few White Russian men spoke even passable English, let alone perfect English.

By reason of custom and, sometimes, necessity, many White Russian women opened dress shops along Avenue Foche in

Little Russia. There they sold their own dresses and the few accessories they carried with them from Russia to Shanghai. The problem they faced with this endeavor, however, was that very few local women could afford to buy the used dresses and accessories, and, when a shop owner did sell an item, she could not afford to replace it with new stock. Eventually, the large number of dress salons originally operated by White Russian women in Shanghai shrunk to very few.

The salvation of the White Russian families were their daughters. These young women — many of whom were attractive and seemed exotic in this new environment because of their unusual spoken accents, manner of dress, and native customs — rescued their families from certain starvation and general destitution by finding employment as singers in cabarets, or as taxi dancers, flower-seller girls, or as nightclub hostesses. These White Russian daughters typically shared their incomes with their families.

The most fortunate White Russian young women — not many — married British or French nationals who were living in Shanghai. But these opportunities steadily dwindled once the entrenched British — who considered marriage to a White Russian woman to be as odious as the marriage of a British citizen to a Chinese woman — began the practice of firing these British husbands from their British-based Shanghai jobs, and then blackballing them from all other employment if they refused to divorce their White Russian wives, rendering these men unemployable and, eventually, destitute.

Alinka had not been immune to the plight of the White Russian immigrant community.

When she was twelve years old, in return for a small payment her parents would receive each month over the next two years, Alinka's father apprenticed her to a British woman named Maggie File. In return, File promised to teach Alinka all she would need to know to become a successful and wealthy courtesan. Alinka, for her part, was required to live with Maggie File, and to obey her every order until she achieved the status of courtesan.

Under this arrangement, once Alinka became a courtesan, and was working regularly in this exalted and envied role, she would share one-third of her income with Maggie File for her first five years as a flower-seller girl.

Alinka, her parents, and Maggie File signed a formal contract in front of a notary public at the British Consulate five days after Alinka's twelfth birthday. One week later, Alinka moved into Maggie File's House of Fragrant Pleasures to begin her training.

CHAPTER 12

IHEARD THE OVERHEAD ELECTRIC WIRES crackling before I ever saw the trolley approaching. Then I saw sparks flying from its screeching, metal wheels as it rounded the corner and pulled into the mid-street station.

I climbed aboard and rode to the Bund. From there, I walked to the House of Multiple Joys. I would begin my investigation by interviewing the house's madam and all the flower-seller girls in her establishment. Meanwhile, as I did that, the SMP's criminalist would collect his evidence and the photographer would document the crime scene. After we finished, the morgue attendant would take away the body.

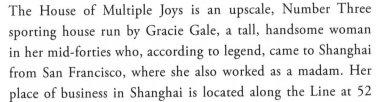

The House of Multiple Joys is an upscale, Number Three sporting house run by Gracie Gale, a tall, handsome woman in her mid-forties who, according to legend, came to Shanghai from San Francisco, where she also worked as a madam. Her place of business in Shanghai is located along the Line at 52 Foochow Road.

Gracie's specialty is providing well-dressed, culturally astute, attractive, and intelligent American women. When she came to Shanghai, she brought several such flower-seller girls with her, and occasionally imported other California girls as needed. Her flower-seller girls, having such names as Big Annie, Singapore Kate, and Lotus-from-California, would ride around Shanghai in their open touring cars when they were not working, setting dress and jewelry styles for Shanghai's other foreign women.

The House of Multiple Joys is one of the last sporting houses to successfully offer upscale American girls to its clientele. This is because the White Russian women, who compete fiercely with the American women, also are beautiful and well-coiffed, but, because of their desperate straits, charge significantly less than their American competitors for the same or better services.

I recall that Gracie once told me that the White Russian women's prices often were so much lower than those charged by her girls that by this year — 1935 — a man in Shanghai could keep a White Russian mistress for a full month at one of their sporting houses for what one night at Gracie's sporting house would cost him.

Gracie ran an efficient and tight operation.

Like most businesses of all types in Shanghai — not only the Flowery Kingdom businesses — Gracie did not deal directly in cash, but took signed chits from her customers, who, if they were local, then were visited at their offices or homes at the end of each month by Gracie's *shroffs* — male Chinese bill collectors. The customers were expected to make full payment to the *shroffs*, and to zero-out their balances each month upon such visits.

In the case of clients who were visiting Shanghai when they took pleasure at a sporting house, they were required to make an arrangement with one of the many chit-bonding companies present in Shanghai. There they would deposit money in return for bonded chits in varying denominations. The visitors used the bonded chits as they would use folding money as they incurred expenses in Shanghai.

Gracie refused to allow drug dealers or out-of-control drug addicts — the latter who she referred to as hopheads — to enter her sporting house, although she occasionally strayed from this standard if the customer was a high-ranking government or military official, a well-known successful retail merchant, a real estate tycoon, or some society celebrity she otherwise knew. For reasons no one seemed to know, however, she never deviated from this policy when it came to wealthy taipans who were addicted to drug use.

Although Gracie's girls were not trained as courtesans, Gracie acted as if they were, and charged her patrons accordingly. To that end, Gracie instructed her flower-seller girls in some of the finer arts of hosting and entertaining, such as serving tea, conversational knowledge of wine and champagne, how to mix and serve alcoholic beverages, important current news events, and the art of engaging in captivating conversation. Several of her girls entertained waiting patrons by playing classical or jazz piano or violin in one of the three ground floor parlors.

The House of Multiple Joys boasted one of the best foreign-language libraries and finest kitchens in the city. Gracie encouraged her customers to visit her sporting house, even if only to use the library or to enjoy a meal prepared by her talented Chinese chef, Fat Lu, who had cooked for the Imperial legation in Peking before our 1911 Revolution overthrew the Manchu Dynasty. His meals were considered social events.

Like most of the madams operating Number Three sporting houses, Gracie, and her customers, too, viewed the sporting houses as important meeting places for male friends and business associates, places where networks were extended, business discussed, and advice dispensed among friends and colleagues.

Gracie encouraged men to unofficially drop by after work, if for no other reason than to have a brandy or to read a newspaper or book located in one of the downstairs parlors, which were furnished with Chinese Chippendale, silk pillows, and oriental rugs.

Gracie once told me, when I asked her about this policy, that making her sporting house familiar to men so that they were comfortable coming there — as if the sporting house was their club — was the best form of marketing she could perform for her business.

CHAPTER 13

ORD CYRIL AVERY BINGHAM, TAIPAN of Markham, Pearson & Preston, a Shanghai-based British counting house — a *hong* — with its home office in London, had been in Shanghai since 1932. He loathed every minute of his time there.

When the day finally would come for him to leave this forsaken Empire outpost and return to England, he intended to liquidate his many real estate holdings in Shanghai, sell his two race horses, convert his savings to gold or silver specie, return to England, quit the Foreign Office, and retire to the English countryside.

"I say, Geoffrey, how do you like your first visit to our club?" Bingham said to his young colleague from Markham, Pearson & Preston.

Geoffrey Parker had recently been transferred from London to Shanghai to begin the three-year-contract period applicable to all Brits working in Shanghai.

"Spot on," his drinking companion said. He lifted his glass of sherry in a mock toast, then sipped his drink.

They were at the famous Long Bar, located on the second

floor of the Shanghai Club, the most exclusive, ultra-snobbish, and notorious British club in Shanghai. The Shanghai Club was known for its exclusivity, its martinis, and its 100-foot-long bar — a bar where birthright meant little, elected peerage meant even less, and local business status meant everything.

When it came to drinking at the Long Bar, it was a man's particular job in Shanghai, and his rank in that job, that dictated where along the bar that man could take his drink. If the club member was a taipan of a major counting house, he could stand and drink at the end of the Long Bar facing nearest the Whangpoo River. If the member was a currency or bullion broker or manager, he could drink next to the taipans, one stop removed from the river view, nearer the center of the bar. Next in line, farther away from the taipans, were the assistant managers of the large counting houses, followed by lesser employees of those *hongs,* and, at the end farthest from the taipans, the men who were temporarily unemployed, but were club members, so long as they still paid their bar bills and club dues.

"Well, Geoffrey, we'll soon fix you up with a membership here," Bingham said. "It's a must, you know, if you plan to do business with the best and only people who matter in Shanghai. You need to club together." He paused to sip his drink.

"The club helps our networks thrive, Old Chap," Bingham said, "puts the right people together in business, and is a must to sustain social contacts among families." He raised his drink and swallowed a sip.

"I look forward to all that," Geoffrey said, as he smiled. He drank a bit of his sherry and furtively glanced around them at the other club members and their nearby guests.

Lord Bingham's face suddenly changed. He frowned as he considered the thought that had just come to him. He leaned in close to his companion.

"To be candid, I don't know how long all this might last," he said. "Don't repeat any of this, Geoffrey," he added, as he looked around to make sure no one else could hear him, "but I don't know how long we'll be able to maintain the club the way it should be kept. I expect things here will begin to change for the worse one of these days."

"What do you mean?" Geoffrey asked. His face contorted, reflecting his concern and puzzlement. He raised his glass to his lips and sipped his sherry, looking over the lip of his glass at his host as he did so.

Bingham moved in closer and spoke in a tone even more hushed than normally required by club rules.

"This isn't for publication, but our membership numbers have drastically declined as more and more men are posted back home to reduce company expenses. It's all because of the worldwide economic Depression caused by those greedy, damned Hebrews working on Fleet Street and Wall Street. The Depression has finally spread to Shanghai, and has steadily increased in intensity.

"The club has had trouble paying its mortgage these last few years because our members' dues-base has drastically shrunken. We've been late many times, and now are behind several months again, with little prospect this time of making up the deficit funds from remaining members' dues."

He paused and gulped down the balance of his drink, then

looked around to be sure he still was not being overheard. He leaned in closer to his drinking companion.

"We've always managed to pull together the money needed for the mortgage-payment deficit, always at the last minute, by assessing our remaining members who still are solvent." He paused to look around again.

"I don't know that we can continue doing that, or if our members will stand for these assessments much longer, or if they even will have the ability to make those payments in this Depression." He shook his head as if reconciling himself to an unhappy fact he'd just uncovered and acknowledged.

Bingham again looked around to make sure his conversation was not being overheard.

"Now, to add to that problem, I've been told that after we refused to admit that playboy, Victor Sassoon, as a new member, he retaliated by purchasing the club's mortgage from the Hong Kong & Shanghai Bank. That notorious Hebrew is now our banker.

"Imagine his impertinence merely because we wouldn't make him a member? Doesn't he know that certain people don't belong in certain places? It's not as if we are picking on Hebrews. Why, we even recently denied membership to the Chinese Prime Minister. Imagine them both wanting to be members of our club." Bingham shook his head in staccato bursts, as if astonished by this concept.

"In any event, Old Boy, who knows what harm that Hebrew might cause us, as our banker now, because we kept him out of the club and kept him in his place?"

Geoffrey shook his head in wonderment. "Damn Hebrews and all their money. They caused the Depression with their flyby-night banks, and they still control everything. No wonder they shouldn't be in a club like this."

He made a clucking noise with his mouth. "What's this world coming to when they can mess with a man's private club?"

If you were a prominent or upper-class British citizen living and working in Shanghai, the Shanghai Club was an essential establishment for you to belong to because it attempted to preserve familiar institutions and amusements for British citizens living there, although London rules were conveniently bent or often ignored altogether, with the consent of the members, to conveniently conform to the local meteorological climate.

The Shanghai Club's physical structure was the most grandiose of the Bund's many extravagant buildings constructed along the waterfront of the Whangpoo River — that one and one-half kilometer strip of Shanghai known locally as the Million-Dollar Skyline. The club's physical plant and ambiance modeled itself after the most exclusive clubs found in London and New York, with its massive white marble façade designed in the neo-classical style.

The club had its Long Bar, its plush stone foyer, wainscoted reading rooms, two plush dining rooms, a fully equipped gas kitchen, and a rooftop pavilion for light-meals and drinks. It also offered its members a card room, a room with snooker and billiard tables, a writing room, a large and opulent ballroom, short-term rental bedrooms, and small, long-term apartments for members in residence. The floors were connected by two elevators, as well as by a sumptuous, wide, curving marble staircase. The entire club premises was air conditioned, a rare luxury in 1930s Shanghai.

The Shanghai Club banned women, Chinese, other non-Caucasians, Catholics, Jews, and several other nationalities from membership. It even prohibited them from coming onto the premises to visit as guests, although wives of members were welcome to participate in club activities and to take advantage of club amenities, even if their husbands were not present, provided the women never left the ground floor.

The club also excluded Caucasian British Empire citizens if they did not have the proper jobs. Caucasian foreigners who held office in any of the large *hongs*, however, even if they were not British citizens, so long as they were not women, Catholic or Jewish, might be invited to membership. Appropriate junior employees of the counting houses, if they were not otherwise a member of some prohibited group, were encouraged to join the club, although their drinking place at the Long Bar might make membership seem remote to them.

The club was not a place a member visited only occasionally. To the British man who had achieved membership, daily attendance was obligatory.

Dressed in their mandatory jackets and ties, taipans, bankers, and other captains of Shanghai industry appeared at the club at least once each weekday to see who was there, to be seen, to catch-up on gossip — both personal and business related — and to make a clear statement that their places in Shanghai's business and social communities remained intact, notwithstanding the Depression.

The daily routine was simple: Most foreigners' business

offices closed at 5:30 p.m. Dinner was taken at 8:00. In between, club members visited the club for the cocktail hour — as it was known — for drinks alone or with their wives in one of the regular bars located on the ground floor, but never with their mistresses — although having a mistress at one time or another was another social requisite of club status, albeit an unstated one.

Because, like most successful British subjects working in Shanghai, Lord Bingham devoted himself as much to play as he did to his business as a taipan, he used the club for general socializing and networking, making business contacts (although under the club's rules business was never conducted on its premises), playing cards, or snooker or billiards, and having drinks.

Away from the club, Bingham attended to his first love, horse racing, and frequented the Shanghai Race Course (on Wei Hai Wei Avenue, near the corner where that street intersected Nanking Road) for occasional pony races. He also attended greyhound races at the Canidrome in the French Concession, and attended *hai alai* matches, also at the Canidrome. Such was the life of a typical taipan in Shanghai.

Beginning in 1933, Lord Bingham served as chairman of the Shanghai Race Club's Champion's Day Race for the prestigious spring and autumn race meets held on the first Saturdays in May and November. On those days, the International Settlement's offices all closed and the various national flags of the International Settlement's major occupants were flown.

Bingham was also a regular patron at the House of Multiple Joys, and used the sporting house much as Gracie Gail hoped.

He engaged in periodic liaisons with its flower-seller girls, and he used the premises as his second-tier club, away from the Shanghai Club, taking an occasional meal there or using its library as a reading room.

Like most wealthy British subjects living in Shanghai, Lord Bingham kept a paid staff to take care of his personal needs. Servants cooked and served his meals and drinks when he ate at home, cleaned his house — which was located along fashionable Avenue Joffre in the French Concession — cleaned and ironed his clothing, and otherwise attended to his personal needs, all for a monthly sum that seemed paltry to Bingham, but which meant a great deal to his Chinese servants.

CHAPTER 14

WHEN I ARRIVED AT THE House of Multiple Joys, a coolie maid took me to the third floor to see the body of the victim. Gracie and several girls were standing in the hallway outside the entertaining room's closed door.

I assumed that neither Gracie nor any of the flower-seller girls had entered the room after the body was discovered. At least I hoped Gracie remembered that much about police work from the brief period when we regularly pillowed together.

As I approached the door, the girls stared at me with predatory, cautious eyes. They moved behind Gracie. Several of the girls with whom I had pillowed at one time or another offered me flirtatious smiles.

Gracie nodded as I approached.

"Good morning, Gracie," I said.

"And to you, too, Inspector Detective," she said, as she smiled at me.

I tilted my head toward the door. "Is this where she's at?"

Gracie nodded again.

"Have the criminalist and photographer been here yet?" I asked.

"There's a man in the entertaining room now," she said,

"but I don't know if he's one of them you mentioned. I don't think I saw a camera with him, just a beat-up grip."

"Wait here with your girls until I call you," I said. "Then I'll need a private room where I can talk to each of you, one at a time."

I opened the door to the entertaining room, but did not enter. I stood in the doorway and looked in. The familiar smell of death slapped me hard. I automatically slipped into observation mode, and quickly glanced around to get a feel for the overall crime scene. Following my usual practice, I now would form initial impressions of the crime scene and the crime, based on my past experiences with other crime scenes, then see if the evidence at this crime scene sustained them.

The room was not the typical Shanghai brothel entertaining bedroom. Not at Gracie's place. All her girls had large rooms with nice furnishings, attractive wallpaper, and well-made — if somewhat worn — oriental rugs scattered around.

Three of the walls of this room had been, sometime in the distant past, painted light blue. The fourth wall was covered with well-worn, flocked, white wallpaper. The bed, dresser, and two chairs also were worn, but were presentable vernacular-country furniture — the type popular, but costly, in the 1920s. A wooden trunk sat against one wall. A red-lacquer kang table stood next to another wall. The third wall framed a four-door A-frame upright cabinet.

What I noticed most was that this sporting house crime scene was far better furnished than I could afford to do for myself in my flat on my meager inspector detective's salary and monthly squeeze.

The flower-seller girl's body was on the floor near the foot of the bed. She was fully clothed, lying on her back.

None of the furniture was upended. The bed was made. There were perfume bottles standing on the dresser. None was knocked over.

The criminalist was packing up his equipment, putting it back into his grip, as I viewed the crime scene from the doorway. He looked over at me.

"Afternoon, Inspector Detective."

"*Ayeeyah*, Dr. Yin. Good afternoon. Finished collecting your dust and other evidence, have you?"

He shook his head. "Indeed, for what it's worth, given how much traffic this room has every day and night. The fingerprints and hair I collected should be useless."

I did not see the photographer. "Has Mr. Fong been here yet?" I asked.

"No. He's on his way. The room's yours, just don't disturb anything Fong might want to photograph. You know how fussy he can be."

I nodded and stepped into the entertaining room after he walked out.

I knelt down and looked under the bed. Nothing. Not even dust balls. I opened the wardrobe door. There were several dresses hanging inside. Nothing was hidden behind them.

Nothing I could see suggested robbery as a motive since the room was undisturbed and apparently had not been searched and upended as I would have expected in the case of a theft.

I leaned over to examine the body.

The woman had dull red hair, was slender, and was far more pale than death alone would have rendered her. She was wearing a flower-embroidered kimono that would have fallen below her knees if she were standing, but, because she was on her back, was pushed up above her thighs exposing her privates. I pulled the hem of the kimono down to cover her. I had no desire to have her exposed while I was there doing my work. I made a mental note to mention this to the photographer or to leave him a note so when he photographed her he could raise her kimono above her thighs to recreate how she was originally found.

The woman's face seemed to be in peaceful repose, although her throat had been cut almost from ear to ear.

Given the condition of the room and the girl's peaceful face, I concluded that either she knew her assailant and had let him into her entertaining room, then had been murdered from behind, completely unaware of her oncoming fate, or that her assailant had secretly entered her room while she'd been away from it, then had surprised her and accosted her from behind.

When I finished looking around, I wrote the note to the photographer, placed it on the body, then decided that this was silly. I pocketed the note and pulled the woman's kimono back up to her thighs where it had been when I first saw her. Then I stepped out into the hallway, closing the door behind me. The room would remain untouched, I hoped, until Fong arrived to perform his photographer's duties at the death scene.

Gracie and the girls looked expectantly at me as I walked up the hallway toward them.

"Gracie," I said, "a minute please." I beckoned with my hand. She then pointed toward a room where we would have privacy.

"Is her room as it was found?" I asked.

Gracie shrugged. "Except for what the bloke who was in there when you arrived might have done to it. Before he arrived, I shooed everyone out and closed the door as soon as I saw the situation."

"Who was her last customer?"

"None tonight. She had a bad cold and had taken the night off."

"I'll need a list of her regulars," I said.

"I'll have it for you before you leave."

"Anything you want to tell me that might be important to my investigation?"

"Only that she didn't have any enemies. Her men loved her, and she got along good with my other girls."

I nodded and made a brief note in my notebook.

"I'll need to talk now with the girl who found her, and then with all the other girls," I said.

"When I'm finished with each girl, have them go somewhere away from here so they cannot talk with the other girls I haven't interviewed yet. That includes you, too, Gracie, when we're done here. No talking to the girls about what we said in here."

"I understand. Are we finished here?" she said, as she stood up from the chair she'd taken when we entered the room.

I also stood up, and nodded. "Send in the girl who discovered the body."

Before she left the room, Gracie reached out and handed me an envelope — this month's squeeze. I took it from her and could feel the thick wad of folding money inside. I put the envelope into my suit-jacket pocket, thanked her, and walked her to the door. Then I awaited the arrival of the flower-seller girl who had discovered the body.

The young woman said she was from Philadelphia, and that they called her Fantastic Filly. She was white, as expected at this Number Three sporting house, American, and was, I guessed, about twenty years old, maybe a year or two more, and very pretty. She told me she played the violin, took lessons regularly at Miss Gracie's insistence, and recently had switched from playing classical music in the parlors, where the men waited, to playing some of the popular Jerome Kern and George Gershwin jazz tunes she'd heard at picture shows.

Once she seemed to be relaxed, I called a halt to her rambling talk and began to ask questions.

"Do you know the names of the customers who visited the dead woman last night?" I asked. I said this even though Gracie had told me the woman hadn't worked last night because she'd had a bad cold. I wanted to see if their stories would be consistent.

The young woman seemed puzzled and shook her head. "I don't think she had any visitors last night. When I was playing the violin in the front parlor, off and on for most of the night, she also sat there, never leaving her chair, sipping a drink.

"I think she had a cold or something else because every time I returned to the parlor, she was sitting there in the same chair, not smiling, looking dazed, red-nosed, and miserable."

"You were the one who found her?" I said.

"Yes, sir. I knocked on her door after we closed up for the night to return a shawl I had borrowed the night before. There was no answer. I thought she might be asleep, so I quietly went into her room to leave the shawl for her. That's when I saw her on the floor."

"If she didn't answer your knock, why didn't you wait until the morning to return the shawl?"

"No reason," she said, "except we go in and out of each other's rooms after hours, even when someone's asleep, unless, of course, you have flagged your door to show you are entertaining a client who is staying over.

"I saw no harm in going in last night since I had her shawl with me as I passed her room, and knew she would be alone because she was sick."

I nodded my understanding and finished up with her. I warned her against talking to the other girls about our discussion until after I left the building. I told her to send in the next flower-seller girl.

Two hours later, having learned nothing new from any of the girls I questioned after I interviewed Fantastic Filly, I took the list of the dead girl's regular customers from Gracie, and headed back to the station house to see what, if anything, the criminalist had found that might be useful. I would also examine Fong's photographs of the crime scene as soon as the lab boys had them ready.

CHAPTER 15

O N THE DAY THAT WAS the fourth anniversary of Sin's arrival at the master's house in Amoy — the day each year the master and Sin arbitrarily celebrated as Sin's birthday since his new life, his rebirth, had started on that day — the master sat with Sin and Hao in the courtyard. The morning was frigid, a soft wind blowing, but neither bare-chested Sin nor bare-chested Hao shivered. They sat on the cold, hard ground, both facing the master, with their legs crossed and heads slightly bowed, as a sign of respect to their teacher.

"You both have progressed well, my sons," the master said, as he looked first at Hao, the eldest son, then at Sin. "I am proud of you both."

"Tomorrow, my sons, is the day we have been working toward these past four years. Tomorrow, you will challenge each other and will fight to the death."

He paused to see if either son would breach discipline and show some reaction to his statement. Neither did. He was pleased, although he did not show it.

"You shall use all the skills and tools I have shared with you. You also may use any method to advantage that appears to you, whether or not I have taught it to you.

"Today and tonight you will continue to be brothers. Tomorrow you will be lethal enemies.

"In the evening, when your combat has finished, one of you and I will celebrate his new life as my assassin."

CHAPTER 16

I WAS STANDING OUTSIDE IN FRONT of the station house smoking and thinking about the murder of the flower-seller girl at the House of Multiple Joys, and, more significantly, about the utter failure of anyone there to be able, or willing, to help me, when a constable stepped outside, waved at me, and said, "The chief inspector wants to see you, sir. Right now."

I returned to my office, took my pistol from the drawer as protocol required, and slipped on my jacket.

"Sit," Chief Inspector Chapman said, not looking up at me as I knocked on the doorsill and then, unbidden, entered his office. I lowered myself into the only unoccupied chair in the cramped office.

The chief inspector finished whatever he'd been doing when I walked in, closed the folder holding some papers I could not read upside down — although I tried — and pushed his chair away from the desk as he looked up.

"We got another one," he said. "Well, not quite another one, Old Chap, but close enough."

I must have looked confused, which I was, because his *not quite another one* statement dashed my understanding of what I expected him to continue saying as he made his statement.

"A body was found this morning at the Temple of Supreme

Happiness. Not a flower-seller girl, though. This time, one of the customers. Garroted by someone." He shook his head as if he found this state of affairs incomprehensible.

"You know that's not so unusual, sir, other than the choice of weapon used," I said, surprised he was making a big deal of it by seeming so grave. "Happens from time-to-time. I suppose you want me to look into it."

"You *suppose* correctly, Inspector Detective. But what I also want is for you to show some enthusiasm for resolving these murders, both of them now," he said, "and some enthusiasm for doing your job like a professional."

I thought that was an odd statement for him to make since he'd taken the opposite position when he first assigned me to the murder at the House of Multiple Joys. Then he wanted me to go through the motions of investigating and to close-down the case as expeditiously as possible, not to make any effort to solve and thereby prolong the case. *What had changed since then?*

I wasn't about to ask him, but would keep my eyes and ears open to see if I could find out from the station's gossip circuit.

"When customers start being put down, it's bad for business. And if it's bad for business, it's bad for Shanghai. Specifically, Inspector Detective, it's then bad for the Council and the SMP, including me and you. Understand?"

Not really, I thought. "Yes, Chief Inspector, I understand."

I understood the concept, in general, but, wondered, *Why would the chief inspector even raise this with me?*

The chief inspector looked hard at me as he said this, had made me uncomfortable, and then added, "Besides, as you know, Sun-jin, customers are harder to replace than dead flower-seller girls so we cannot permit anything to occur and continue that might scare them away."

"Yes, sir," I said, feigning enthusiasm and nodding my head several times to convey this. "I fully understand."

I rode the electric streetcar to the end of the Bund. I walked past the Baby Wall and the Public Garden to Chapei in the Old City, then walked to the corner of Dun and Haosung Roads, over to the Number Three sporting house known as the Temple of Supreme Happiness.

This was the area of Shanghai that used to be in part of the treaty-port area formerly known as the American Settlement. Chapei, my home district, became part of the International Settlement when the Americans and British merged their treaty territories.

Chapei is heavily populated by Chinese who both live and work there. We Celestials treat the Old City as a Chinese protectorate, and jealously guard our self-created prerogatives there.

The Chinese in Chapei maintain special sporting houses that employ only Chinese women. These sporting houses, however, service all nationalities. I had never been in the Temple of Supreme Happiness, either officially or otherwise, so I was curious about it.

But I wasn't comfortable visiting there, not even officially, because of the danger it offered me. I hoped that when the Chinese SMP's inspector detective showed up, I would already be back at my office in the Settlement so I would not have to explain to him my presence in Chapei or at the Chapei murder scene. I didn't want either to be shot or arrested by the Chinese

SMP, in spite of the existence of the Compact, which afforded me, as it did other Settlement SMP policemen, little comfort.

Like many of the old mansions in Chapei, the Temple of Supreme Happiness was well maintained — at least on the outside — and was imposing with its tall columns bracketing a pair of seven-foot high wooden-entrance doors. Interestingly, because I'd had no reason to anticipate this based on my experience at other sporting houses, unlike many similar mansions used as brothels, this one appeared to be as impressive and well preserved when seen in sunlight as it likely would seem under streetlights, after dark.

I walked up the twelve brick steps onto a wide, wrap-around wooden porch, and used the heavy brass door-knocker to announce my presence outside. The sporting house's front door, like the front doors of all sporting houses operating in Shanghai, had the mandatory red lantern hanging above the door, and also displayed the names of the flower-seller girls who worked there on a cardboard sheet posted to the entrance's right side.

The door opened almost immediately.

I stepped into a foyer and was taken to a first floor, richly appointed parlor. Once there, I showed my warrant card ID to the elderly, servant woman who had admitted me, and stated that I wanted to see the madam of the house. I glanced around while the woman went to fetch her.

The parlor was decorated in mixed styles of Victorian and Art deco. Everything I could see — chairs, tables, wallpaper, rugs, and wall-hangings — looked well-cared for. I knew, however, based on other bordellos I'd seen, that although this same care would be present in other rooms on this lower floor, the upper-levels and entertaining rooms would likely be shabby, would need painting or wallpaper repairs or replacements, and would have worn, cast-off furniture that had seen better days on level one, but were now doing duty upstairs.

The long, hanging strings of beads that covered a door across the room rattled, and a middle-aged woman walked through them into the parlor. I assumed she either was the house's madam, the person I'd requested to meet with, or she was the house's official *Amah*, and I was being brushed-off. I'd soon know.

Her name was Li Suh-wang. She was the madam and owner of the Temple of Supreme Happiness.

Suh-wang ran an upscale flowery-kingdom sporting house that employed girls known as *Number Threes* — top-level women to whom the customers paid three Shanghai silver dollars to share a drink, and then paid much more, negotiated on a case-by-case basis, to have sex with afterward. This pricing formula differentiated an upscale Number Three house, such as this sporting house and the House of Multiple Joys, from a lower-scale Number Two house, which was populated by women who charged only two Shanghai silver dollars for a drink, and another, fixed-price, three Shanghai silver dollars for their bodies. The age and quality of the women who worked in each type of sporting house were reflected in the two different pricing formulae in the appropriate-level house.

I quickly learned from my conversation with Li Suh-wang that she was not middle-aged, as I had mistakenly thought. She was young, having retired from working as a flower-seller girl at the ripe-old age of twenty-six to open her own sporting house. I guessed she now was thirty-four or thirty-five, although she looked considerably older. Such was life in the Flowery Kingdom.

"*Ayeeyah!* Welcome to the Temple of Supreme Happiness on this inauspicious occasion," she said, as she approached me.

Inauspicious? I wondered what ill-luck or misfortune she thought my visit foreshadowed, other than the fact that no one liked the police to officially visit their sporting house, not even friendly police.

"*Heya – Hello*," I said. "I am here about the body found this morning. I have some questions."

I did not disclose that I already knew a few of the details of its discovery, facts I had learned from Chief Inspector Chapman. I wanted to see how much information Suh-wang would voluntarily disclose to me and if that information would be truthful.

I asked what she knew about the discovery of the client's body. I also asked for the name of the girl who had serviced and found him. She answered my questions without hesitation.

"I'll want to talk to the girl who found him, and then to the girl he was here to see, if they are different women."

"Same flower-seller girl, not two," Suh-wang said. "I bring her to you now."

"Take me to the body first, Auntie," I said, as I bowed slightly, "and wait with me until I have finished with it. I'll see the girl afterward."

We walked up the steps to the fourth floor landing, and down a darkened hallway to the second door on the left.

The door was wide open. There were two constables inside, one photographer (not Fong, but another staff member I'd seen around the station house but didn't know), Dr. Yin, the criminalist, and someone from the morgue, all waiting for me to arrive so they could preliminarily report to me and wrap-up their work. I made them wait while I looked around, silently taking in the whole scene.

The body was that of a male, about forty to fifty years old. He was fully dressed and stretched out on his back on the floor, lying on a throw rug. His eyes bulged in death. His face was a pasty blue shade. Blood had dried in the corner of his mouth.

Based on what I'd been told by Chief Inspector Chapman, the man was the taipan of the counting house Smith, Boone & Sons — a large, successful *hong* based in Hong Kong, with an active office in Shanghai. That struck me as odd since a taipan, if he wanted to pillow with a flower-seller girl, surely could afford an exalted courtesan in the privacy of one of Shanghai's luxurious hotels, where he could order fine wine, an exquisite meal for two, and have room service deliver opium to them. A taipan would not have to resort to a sporting house, not even to an upscale, Number Three sporting house, to pillow.

Dr. Yin looked up as I walked in. He nodded. I walked over to him and knelt down beside him and the body. Suh-wang stood outside the doorway, in the hallway, watched by a constable I'd assigned to keep her there. I didn't want her to wander away and talk to any of the flower-seller girls about the questions I had asked her.

"Homicide or natural?" I said.

I always felt silly asking this. It was a stupid question, of course, since I had been summoned there as a homicide inspector detective. But our formal SMP procedure required that I ask the question and that the criminalist answer it. Then we both would check off that box as part of our reports of our meeting. Such was the silly life, sometimes, of Shanghai's crime fighters.

"He was strangled," Yin said. "No, actually, he was garroted. Death was pretty quick."

"Time of death?" I asked.

"Four to ten hours ago. I'll be more specific when we've looked at him back at the laboratory."

"I'll need the usual from you," I said.

"Right." He nodded.

I wondered if the Chinese SMP force had been called, and, if so, why they hadn't arrived yet. I wanted to finish my work before they got here so I could leave Chapei. It was one thing to live in the Old City, as I have all my life, and be accepted as a resident. It was another matter to be an SMP inspector detective and to trespass on the Chapei police force's territory.

I looked around the room, but did not see anything unusual. I walked downstairs, followed by Suh-wang. She set me up in a side room with the flower-seller girl who had found the body.

The woman pretty much repeated what Suh-wang had told me. She had serviced the client without any problems from him. Afterward, while he was dressing, she left the room in her robe to go down the hall to use the bidet and commode. She was gone about fifteen minutes. When she returned, she found her client on the floor, on his back, fully dressed. She thought he had fainted and tried to revive him, but then saw the ligature marks on his throat. She ran and found Suh-wang, who returned with her to the entertaining room.

A few minutes after that, the flower-seller girl told me, while she stood by and listened, Suh-wang went out into the hallway to use the telephone attached to the wall. Suh-wang, the woman told me, had called the International Settlement SMP, rather than the local Chapei police, because Suh-wang knew that the customer, who was a regular at the sporting house, was a taipan, an important man in the Settlement.

That answered one question for me, and I relaxed, no longer worried about the Chapei police showing up while I was there. I told Suh-wang to call the Chapei SMP twenty minutes after I left.

I returned to the station house, then went to Chief Inspector Chapman's office to report to him, as he had ordered me to do when he assigned me to the case.

CHAPTER 17

SIN AND HAO STOOD TEN meters apart in the courtyard staring at one another. Each had a grim look on his face. They were bare-chested and barefoot, clad only in loose fitting, ankle-length *Wing Chun* sparring pants. Both young men had oiled their bodies to give themselves an advantage and an equal disadvantage in the hand-to-hand combat to follow. Each had several ancient weapons of his choice spread out on the ground behind him.

Sin's array of weapons included a garrote with two wires, a short-handled axe, and a two-edge, broad knife. Hao's weapons were a curved dagger, a steel chain with a steel ball on its end — containing razor-sharp spikes protruding from its surface — and a short sword.

"Approach me," the master said to Sin. Then he turned to Hao and uttered the same instruction. He stood between the boys.

"I will step away from you in one moment and will drop this owl's feather," he said, extending his hand so both his sons could see the object.

"When the feather touches the ground, your combat will begin. Not before. If either of you commences too soon, I will step in and terminate him.

"You will engage in combat until one of you dies. You will not have rest or respite until that has occurred.

"When you have begun your combat, I will leave the courtyard and lock all doors into the house. I will return at sunrise. If there are two of you living when I return, I will slay you both and begin my training again with two other young boys. Only one of you may be standing when I return in the morning."

That said, the master lifted the owl's feather above his head, looked first at Sin and then at Hao, then released the plume.

Both boys stared at the feather as it descended to the ground, drifting side-to-side, riding a slight breeze.

CHAPTER 18

Chief Inspector Chapman looked up as I walked into his office to report to him. He waved me over to the chair in front of his desk.

"What did you find out?" he said, referring, I assumed, to my trip to the Temple of Supreme Happiness.

"Nothing beyond what the criminalist could see from his visual inspection," I said. "I'll wait to learn if the autopsy gives anything new. Then I'll go back and question the madam and girls again."

"Be a good chap, Old Man, and stay on top of this. The Council is watching how we handle this. The two killings might be a coincidence, but maybe not."

"I wanted to talk to you about that, sir," I said.

Chapman looked sharply at me, a frown on his face, as if he anticipated what I was about to say. "What about?"

"I'd like to be reassigned from these cases. My heart's not in them."

"What are you talking about, Inspector Detective? What kind of nonsense is this?"

The chief inspector clearly was angry.

I took a deep breath. "I'm finding it hard to get up any enthusiasm for solving the two crimes. They seem pretty routine. You should put a greenhorn sub-inspector on them, not a seasoned inspector detective.

"Someone," I said, "with less experience than me. Some rookie." I paused for the chief inspector's reaction. He didn't say anything, but his face darkened as I watched.

"Besides," I said, "the girls and customers know the risks they engage in. It comes with the business."

You might have thought I slapped the chief inspector in his face. He abruptly sat up straighter and stiffened. His eyes narrowed.

"Are you too good, too *seasoned*," he said, drawing out the word, I assumed, to be sure I caught his repetition of my use of the word, as well as his sarcasm, "to handle routine homicides?"

I took a deep breath and said nothing.

"You'll be off these cases and back walking a constable's beat on the streets if that's your attitude, Inspector Detective." He paused briefly while he looked down to light his pipe.

When he'd sufficiently puffed the tobacco stuffed into the bowl to ignite it, he looked up at me again.

"You will work these cases, Inspector Detective, giving them your best and fullest attention, as with any case I assign you. You do not get to pick your assignments. I do that."

"Yes, sir, Chief Inspector."

I purposely assumed an embarrassed and sorrowful expression on my face in an attempt to regain some measure of favor with the chief inspector. It seemed to work because he stopped frowning.

"Sun-jin," he said, now using an unusually friendly tone of voice, "I know you see the world as black vs. white, as all good vs. all evil, but you must grow up and stop doing that if you want to continue as an inspector detective. Your view of the world is too rigid, too narrow to help you in your investigations. You are too old to still view the world in such a childish way.

"The world we work in, Sun-jin, is gray. Someone can be a good person who does bad things occasionally or might be a bad person who occasionally does something good. That is the way the world works, Old Boy, especially in Shanghai. The same applies to flower-seller girls, their employers, and to their clients, even clients who are dead taipans."

"I know, sir, but—"

"No *but*, Sun-jin." He paused, then said, "Pay attention to this. The Municipal Council is sensitive to how these murders might affect business for the *hongs* and how they might slow tourism to the city.

"The Council does not want to see its licensing fees and tax collections drop-off because people are afraid to visit the sporting houses," he said.

"It's worried, too, about the loss of revenue from the nearby businesses that flourish and are supported by the flower-seller girls and the sporting houses — the tailors, dress shops, jewelry stores, embroidery shops, restaurants, and food stalls, among others."

I shrugged my indifference. Probably not the smartest thing I've done.

"Sir, if I may say so, the Council is just a group of taipans and other rich businessmen whose only interest is their own special interests, and how those special interests can line their own pockets."

The chief inspector sucked in a deep breath as I finished saying this. His face darkened again, much deeper this time.

"That's insubordination, Inspector Detective."

"Yes, sir. Sorry."

Faced with the chief inspector's unassailable, logical position, I assumed a contrite expression.

"Yes, sir," I said again, but with some sincerity in my tone this time.

"I'll stay with the cases and solve them," I added, as I contorted my face into a false construction I hoped conveyed both enthusiasm and sincerity, flexibility, and good attitude, but not my true feelings about working these cases.

CHAPTER 19

T WELVE-YEAR-OLD ALINKA, MISSING HER PARENTS, and feeling great trepidation concerning the new life she was about to embark on, and certainly not knowing what to expect from Maggie File, resolved to work hard, obey Maggie File, and become the most successful courtesan possible.

She moved into Maggie File's House of Fragrant Pleasures, and was given a private room where she would be expected to live, sleep, and study.

Maggie File turned out to be both a good substitute parental figure for Alinka and a strict, but fair, teacher of the ways of the Flowery Kingdom.

Early on in Alinka's training, Maggie File told Alinka that her eventual sexual duties as a courtesan would be light, but that they would have to be performed according to the highest standards of the profession. She explained that the day would come, if Alinka learned her lessons well, when her defloration would be offered to the highest bidder. As part of this goal, she said, the winning bidder would be required to engage in an elaborate and customary courtship ritual before being permitted to enter Alinka's untested jade gate.

"In the meantime," File said, "you must prepare yourself for your role by studying conversation, acting, music, the martial art known as *Kobudo*, and several languages."

Alinka's days passed quickly at the House of Fragrant Pleasures. She spent her mornings studying Mandarin Chinese and Shanghainese *Hu*, learning English, and learning to play the piano and Chinese lute. She spent part of her afternoons studying the special Chinese accent of women from Soochow, a dialect many men found to be beautiful and soothing, and, therefore, the preferred language spoken by their courtesans.

Alinka was a dedicated and able student. She frequently practiced conversation and social skills with her teacher and another student. She learned to care for her skin, learned how to create various hair styles, and learned, too, how to select the appropriate clothing to wear for various occasions. She also learned to use a jeweler's loop to evaluate precious stones.

Alinka found that acquiring the special social skills required of a courtesan was the most difficult accomplishment of all for her since she had been used to pleasing only her parents, especially her father — an easy audience — up to this time. Now she studied the many ways to please men with whom she would have little or no acquaintance.

After fifteen months of intensive training, Maggie File decided that thirteen-plus-year-old Alinka was ready to embark on the sexual component of her training.

The House of Fragrant Pleasures was the perfect laboratory for these lessons because its flower-seller girls maintained an active clientele of wealthy British and Chinese patrons. The mansion's physical plant also was useful for this purpose, having public rooms that were spacious and, like all high-class bordellos, were beautifully furnished on the first floor.

But that was only on its surface.

Behind the scenes, the mansion had been constructed as a visual laboratory to be used to instruct aspiring, young courtesans in the art of sex and in other skills required to please clients.

Behind the walls on all floors, there existed a warren of poorly lit hallways with peepholes in the walls through which Maggie File and her courtesans-in-training could secretly observe established courtesans at their entertaining and sexual practices, thereby enabling these budding, young courtesans to learn their trade from skilled, visual examples in practice.

Although Alinka excelled in most aspects of her training, the part of her education she enjoyed most were the acting lessons. It was in these classes that she learned to twist her face and body, as well as her smile, to express differing emotions, so she could play whatever role the moment and the client called for.

"Convincing acting," Maggie File said to Alinka, "is a very important part of being a successful courtesan."

Alinka nodded, but said nothing, just as she'd been taught.

"Acting is essential because that is when you create the erotic, fantasy world your client expects," File said, "to take him away from his stressful world of business.

"Through acting," she added, "you will create a make-believe universe for your client where he will imagine himself as a young lover of a beautiful and accomplished young girl."

The day came when Maggie File told Alinka she must choose a new name as her working name. After much thought, Alinka chose the Russian name Natalia. From that day forward, everyone at the House of Fragrant Pleasures referred to Alinka as Natalia, never again calling her by her birth-name.

Courtesans in Shanghai, unlike those working in Hong Kong and other cities in China, found themselves in a looser, more fluid social situation than those women who worked in other parts of the Celestial Kingdom. In Shanghai, the courtesans were permitted to move about freely in public, and were not expected to live a life of seclusion, as they were required to do in Hong Kong and other cities.

In Shanghai, because these women serviced the wealthiest of the Flowery Kingdom's clients, they could, if prudent, accumulate great wealth for themselves before they retired from the business, usually around the age of thirty to thirty-five, and were admired as self-made and successful businesswomen. They often were able to live out their end-days in independence, luxury, and comfort.

When Alinka reached her fourteenth birthday, Maggie File decided she was ready to be deflowered. In accordance with long-accepted practice, File offered Alinka to the highest bidder among a few wealthy men who were invited to vie for the honor of being the first man to enter Alinka.

His name was Bing Wu-li. He was a forty-three-year-old Hong Kong comprador for the trading house Jardine, Matheson & Company, Hong Kong's largest and most successful *hong*. He had outbid the other suitors.

To become Alinka's first client, to enjoy her maidenhood, Wu-li, along with Natalia, now would be required to follow certain time-established courting rituals, all closely supervised by Maggie File.

First, Wu-li would have to be formally introduced to Alinka (but as Natalia, not as Alinka) by some other, well-known client of the House of Fragrant Pleasures. Once that had been accomplished, Wu-li would sit with Maggie File and Natalia in mid-afternoon to drink tea — tea served by one of the women who worked at the sporting house — eat fruit, and make small-talk with the two women.

After some conversation, Natalia would be expected to express her acceptance of Wu-li by directly serving tea to him. That accomplished, the courtship ritual would end, not to be resumed for five days.

When the wooing rite resumed on the fifth day, Wu-li would embark on the next stage required to become the first man to enter Natalia's jade gate.

First, he would give Maggie File a large sum of money to be used to buy Natalia a new wardrobe and to furnish her entertaining room. A portion of the sum, in an amount previously agreed to by Maggie File and Wu-li, would be retained by Maggie File for her own account. The balance of the money would go to Natalia, who would use some portion of it to fix-up her entertaining room in accordance with Wu-li's expressed desires. She would be permitted to keep any money left over once she'd satisfactorily completed this aspect of her role.

Natalia enjoyed spending her share of Wu-li's money required to furnish her entertaining room according to the criteria Wu-li had described to Maggie File. This required that the furnishings be a mixture of Chinese vernacular-country antiques and current Art deco styles, Wu-li's favorites.

Then last, as part of the courting ritual, Wu-li, in order to gain face, would be required to host three expensive dinners at the House of Fragrant Pleasures, one dinner to follow the others into the late night. The three dinners were to be held on the same evening that Wu-li would deflower Natalia.

After the last of the three dinners, which would end well past 2:00 a.m. if everything went in accordance with custom, Wu-li and Natalia would retire to a fantasy-themed room that had been prepared for them for this special occasion in accordance with Wu-li's expressed desires he'd made to Maggie File when they negotiated the terms of the transaction.

There, in the theme room, Wu-li and Natalia would enter into a fantasy garden of make-believe flowers, shrubs, and trees — some painted on the walls, some strewn around the room.

Upon entering the fantasy-theme room, in accordance with custom, Wu-li would court Natalia as if he was her young lover — a man of letters, not a businessman — and would read her poetry written by Li Shang-Yin and other Tang Dynasty romantic poets, all in accordance with centuries-old prescribed ritual.

Natalia played her role superbly, and Wu-li soon entered Natalia's jade gate and took her maidenhood. They then made love many times until, by dawn, Wu-li and Natalia were exhausted and slept soundly in each other's arms.

CHAPTER 20

NANKING-BORN CHEN BAO TOOK HIS duties as comprador very seriously.

In this role, Chen Bao acted as the exclusive intermediary between the European-based counting house he worked for and Chinese businesses in Shanghai.

Chen Bao not only successfully conducted business on behalf of the *hong* that employed him, but, using much flattery and deceit, he left his taipan with the impression that the taipan was the brains behind the *hong*'s success, when all Chen Bao's taipan actually had done to assure the success of his counting house was to have hired Chen Bao as his comprador. Chen Bao was what the Manchus had called the power behind the throne.

To achieve his lofty role as comprador, Chen Bao, like all compradors, was required to read, write, and speak Shanghainese (including the base *Hu* dialect), Mandarin, Cantonese, and English. He also read, wrote, and spoke sufficient French to get along in that language.

In his handling of the business affairs of the *hong*, all business passed through Chen Bao's hands so that he became his taipan's indispensable, de facto, trading partner, all in accordance with the practices of the times.

In this aspect of his duties, Chen Bao frequently took a

personal financial position — often involving monetary risk to him — as part of the typical duties of a comprador. This required that he supply the company with working capital (at interest rates he alone determined), paid for each ship's cargo insurance until the cargo was stored in the taipan's *godown* — *warehouse* — and that he handle the finances for each transaction. In this manner, Chen Bao, like all successful compradors, became very wealthy.

It was not unusual in Shanghai to have a taipan and his trading company, many of whom were deeply in debt — perhaps even on the edge of bankruptcy — employ a comprador who was extremely wealthy. In those situations, it also was not unusual for the comprador to loan money to the taipan for his personal account, or to loan money to the trading company, in return for crippling high-interest payments on the outstanding loan balances, and often in return for equity shares in the *hong*.

This financial relationship meant that the comprador and taipan developed two unusual relationships at the same time — that of employer/employee and that of debtor/creditor. In this situation, certain roles and duties evolved over time. The comprador would pay the wages of the company's Chinese staff, and in turn would receive interest from the trading company for those wages. He also handled all the trading company's cash. He made all sales to and all purchases from Chinese vendors, guaranteed all accounts from his own assets, and made all collections. He also financed the purchase of cargos to be imported and exported.

A taipan never concerned himself with day-to-day business matters, but, instead, devoted his time to leisure — at his club, at the Shanghai Race Course, with his mistress, and for a few hours each trading day, at his desk at the *hong's* office, making a show of being useful and busy.

Chen Bao and his taipan, while traditional in most of the comprador's and taipan's ways of life, were not traditional in their financial affairs, business operations, or personal relationship. True, Chen Bao performed the usual tasks of the comprador, tasks that greased the path of the *hong* in its dealings with the Chinese. And thus, in that regard, Chen Bao was indispensable to his *hong* and his taipan. But, unlike many other compradors, Chen Bao did not become the personal banker of his taipan or for his taipan's trading company for Chen Bao's taipan did not allow this type of relationship to emerge. Chen Bao's taipan understood that power resided with those who held the purse.

This anomalous relationship meant that there had to be trade-offs made by Chen Bao's taipan and Chen Bao in order for this particular comprador/taipan arrangement to successfully exist. Thus it was that Chen Bao's taipan, to retain Chen Bao as his comprador, and not have him move to more lucrative pastures, looked the other way when Chen Bao skimmed cash from various accounts, charged higher interest on working capital and insurance than most compradors charged, and when Chen Bao inflated the records of his staffs' salaries above the amount he actually paid them so he could pocket the spread.

This loose arrangement, Chen Bao's taipan had decided early on, was a small cost to incur to do business successfully in Shanghai through one of the port's shrewdest compradors.

CHAPTER 21

LEFT THE CHIEF INSPECTOR'S OFFICE and went to my desk to think over how I should approach the investigation.

Duly infused with my new, internally mandated (but feigned) enthusiasm for the investigation, and also instilled with a firm desire to remain employed by the SMP as an inspector detective rather than be demoted back to the level of foot-patrol constable, I decided to try an unusual approach to crime solving in Shanghai. I would visit the undisputed ruler of Shanghai's underworld, Big-Eared Tu.

All Shanghai — including the self-absorbed Japanese in the Hongkew — respected Tu's opinions and desires. They had no choice. Nor would I. Whatever advice Tu might offer me, I would not take lightly.

No one in Shanghai — not even the Municipal Council which collected hefty licensing fees and taxes from the sporting houses and their related off-shoot businesses, or even Generalissimo Chiang Kai-shek, who was reputed to receive substantial revenue from the sporting houses to use in the Kuomintang's fight against the Communists — had a greater interest in maintaining the level of income produced by the flower-seller houses than did Tu. It was rumored that his personal financial take from the sporting houses far exceeded the licensing fees and taxes received by the Municipal Council or the squeeze received by Chiang Kai-shek from the Flowery Kingdom operations.

Perhaps, I thought, *I could enlist Tu's help — including his vast connections throughout Shanghai's underworld — in solving the murders and preventing others. That certainly would be good for my personnel file at headquarters.*

I had only talked with Tu once before. That was when I was still a foot-patrol constable and had stopped by one afternoon to visit Sun-yu at a nightclub where he then worked as the club's manager. Big-Eared Tu was at the club with several of his pupils — as he referred to his henchmen — discussing some matter Eldest Brother later refused to tell me about. Tu wasn't yet the significant power in Shanghai he would become, and I knew very little about him at the time.

What I most remembered about Tu from that time was how physically unattractive he was, and how, in particular, his enormous, protruding ears caused my staring eyes to lock onto them, making me fear that he would catch me doing so.

I also recalled that when Tu looked at me that time at that nightclub, I sensed cruelty in his eyes and heard a knife's edge in his brief spoken greeting to me.

I was to learn much about Tu as the years passed. Frankly, I became impressed by his achievements, even though most of them were unlawful. In many ways, I admired the man, although I would not admit that to anyone or in public. Certainly not to any of my colleagues at the station house.

Big-Eared Tu's genius was that he was able to take traditional Chinese spheres of influence and apply modern,

1930s business methods to them. He recognized that what was required to make Shanghai work for his benefit was the forging of economic bonds among the city's underworld, its police, its politicians, the traditionally wealthy Chinese who lived in Shanghai, the warlords who governed the coast of China, and, most of all, Chiang Kai-shek, who had, with his wife, Soong Mai-ling, brought about the New Life Reform Movement in the city. To this understanding of circumstances, Tu applied vision, supreme cunning, ruthlessness, and his persuasive, if often coercive, skills as a negotiator.

Having formulated his approach to consolidating his power in the city, Tu made his first move by penetrating the closely held ranks of the various warlords who controlled the opium trade in Shanghai, and, specifically in Frenchtown. He decided he would consolidate that trade under one entity that he formed and controlled, an entity he called the Constancy Society. That entity was wholly-owned by the Green Gang.

Tu initiated his power play by ousting Pock-Marked Huang and replacing him with himself as the Green Gang's leader and head of the Constancy Society.

Tu used the Constancy Society and the Green Gang unlike anyone in China had used a triad before him. Unlike Pock-Marked Huang, who had viewed the Green Gang as an old-fashioned secret society that was mostly social and benevolent, Tu applied 1930s, innovative corporate business concepts to the triad, making the Green Gang the equivalent of a corporate holding company which controlled the Constancy Society. Each drug warlord, under Tu's plan, had a membership in the Constancy Society, and pledged his sole allegiance to Big-Eared

Tu. Those warlords who refused to fall in line with Tu's plan soon found themselves, instead, falling into graves.

This approach worked well for Tu. He initially organized and controlled all of the opium activity in the French Concession, south of L'Avenue Eduard VII and west of Mohawk Road. Soon after that, he took over all of the opium trade in the remaining portions of Shanghai. By 1929, Tu had become the undisputed ruler of Shanghai's underworld.

I rode the electric streetcar to its stop on Rue Wagner, a wide, boulevard-like avenue in the French Concession. The street was lined with mature willow trees on both sides. I then walked from the streetcar stop to Tu's three-story brick house. I had telephoned him earlier to make an appointment to meet with him.

An elderly man in servant's livery met me at the door and led me into the Great Room where Tu was seated. Tu stood up and bowed slightly as I walked in.

I furtively glanced around the room as I quickly walked across its expanse to join Tu.

Although he dressed himself in traditional Chinese scholar's clothing — in this instance a coral-color silk gown that buttoned at his neck and fell to his ankles, suggesting the strong Confucian influence in his life — Tu's Great Room was an uneasy stew of traditional Chinese artists' and scholars' furnishings and small table-top artifacts, some Art deco pieces, several European wall hangings, some scattered Oriental rugs, several stiff Chinese yoke-back chairs, and four hanging cages holding his lucky crickets and songbirds.

The décor struck me as an unlikely alliance of cultures and

current trends. I would not have expected this from someone who otherwise seemed so traditional.

"*Heya! — Hello!* Welcome to my home, Inspector Detective. You honor me with your presence." Tu bowed his head slightly in the traditional Confucian manner.

"Thank you, Master Tu," I said. "The honor is mine. I appreciate your willingness to allow me to visit with you on such short notice."

This ritual continued for another few minutes until both Tu and I were silently satisfied we had met our respective Confucian and Taoist obligations of propriety and respect. Then we settled down to business.

"I have come to ask for your help, Master Tu." I described the two murder cases I was investigating.

Tu, who undoubtedly already knew about them since he reputedly knew everything of importance that went on in Shanghai, never acknowledged he was familiar with the crimes.

When I finished, Tu said, "Why do you think I can assist you with these matters?"

It was time again for me to engage in the required Confucian ritual of enhancing — and certainly not doing anything to impair — Tu's face.

Under the long-established rules of decorum practiced by Confucians, I couldn't just say to Tu that because he was the most powerful criminal in Shanghai, and because he had his fingers in everything untoward that went on in the city, that he should be able to put an end to the killings if he wanted to.

Such a statement by me would cause Tu to lose face by obliquely suggesting he had allowed a bad situation to occur in the first place, then had permitted it to continue even though he'd had the power to have prevented and then stopped it.

Such an affront to Tu by such a suggestion clearly was a situation I had no desire to engage in. So, instead, I said the same thing, but attempted to be more circumspect in my choice of words and with my delivery.

"I think you can help me, Master Tu, although perhaps without justifiable warrant for me to think so, because your vast web of associates throughout the city, at all levels, has more resources available to it, and far more contacts from whom to obtain information, than we, the police, have."

Tu remained impassive, betraying no response to my flattering statement. To do otherwise would have caused him to lose face with me. It was as if he'd not heard me speak.

I sat silent, waiting for him to say something, waiting for a full half-minute before he responded.

"Why would I want to help you, Mr. Policeman, if even I could?" Tu said, engaging in his own face-saving statement. He could not come right out and admit to me that he actually did have the power I suggested he had. That, too, in its own way, would be an egregious breach of Confucian etiquette.

He shifted slightly in his seat. "These two unfortunate murders appear unrelated and trivial overall," he said. He crossed his arms at his waist and slid his hands up into the two, wide sleeves of his gown.

I had anticipated this statement and was ready with my response.

"Trivial for now, Master Tu, but not if the killings continue. Eventually, more murders, should they occur, will harm the business of the sporting houses, as well as the related opium business, and will undermine the New Life Reform Movement and Generalissimo Chiang's fund-raising efforts as he fights to drive the Communists from Shanghai. All that, in turn, will financially harm the city, and will, therefore, harm you. It is in both our interests to bring a prompt end to this by working together."

Tu said nothing in response to my assertion. He rang a tiny bell that had been sitting on the arm of his chair. When a servant appeared, Tu ordered tea for us.

He continued to say nothing until the tea arrived, had been poured, and the servant had left the room. Tu sipped his tea, looking at me all the while. He was a study in Taoist patience and tacit Confucian manipulation.

"*Ayeeyah!*" he finally said. "I agree that if these killings continue, there will be some decrease in sporting house business, but overall the loss will be petty.

"As for the sale of opium, hopheads are hopheads. They will buy their dope wherever they can, whether or not at a sporting house or through hotel room service. It is not important.

"In due course, the killings will end and all related business will regain its former level. It is just a matter of time until these matters cease. Neither I nor Chiang's New Life Reform Movement will be harmed in the long run."

Tu's indifference did not surprise me. I had known when I came here that my efforts were, at best, a long shot. But I wasn't yet ready to give in to his studied indifference. I would try a different approach with him although I held no illusions concerning the likelihood of its success.

"A young woman has lost her life," I said, "and one man, too, a patron of a sporting house. Surely that must concern you."

I said this while straining to maintain a straight face, knowing that this man, who reputedly has ordered the deaths of hundreds of people, wouldn't care about two more people who had been murdered.

"Why should I care?" he asked. "No one cares about those women. Such is the life of a flower-seller girl. These women are easily replaced.

"As for the man, he should have known the risk his behavior might entail when he visited the flower-seller girl." He paused a beat, then said, "I am sorry, Inspector Detective, but I will not help you."

He paused briefly, then said, "Good luck." With that he stood up, signaling that it was time for me to leave.

I wasn't surprised by Tu's response, although I had hoped he would have been a little more forthcoming.

I walked out of Tu's home feeling that my futile effort to enlist his aid had been indirectly rewarded. Although Tu would not help me solve the crimes — he'd made that much clear to me — he had not suggested he would stop my investigation or would otherwise oppose it. That counted for a lot. For that reason, I considered my meeting with Tu to have been a success.

As I left Tu's home, I decided that since I already was in Frenchtown, I would pay a goodwill visit to Eldest Brother at his nightclub before returning to my office.

CHAPTER 22

A S THE MASTER STEPPED AWAY from between them, Sin and Hao watched the owl's feather float delicately toward the ground, riding the soft morning current that blew across the courtyard. Both boys, mindful of the master's warning, resisted the urge to retrieve a weapon. They stood stone still.

As the feather touched the ground, Sin and Hao simultaneously leaped backwards, away from the other, never taking their eyes from the other's eyes. They grabbed weapons from the ground and set their stances as they prepared to engage.

The boys walked in a counterclockwise circle, maintaining their distances from one another, each taking the measure of the other. This was how the eleven-year-old and twelve-year-old had been trained over the past years to begin a lethal encounter, a match with an enemy.

Sin held the short axe in his right hand, and slowly arced it back and forth, left to right, in front of him, then back again, feeling the balance and heft of the weapon he knew so well, but had never before used with lethal intent. His left hand remained free.

Hao held his short sword in his left hand and his curved dagger in his right, both at waist level.

The boys continued to slowly walk counterclockwise as if the opening of their contest had been choreographed and rehearsed many times, as in fact it had been, albeit with different adversaries in mind.

Hao, without breaking eye contact or offering Sin any other warning, suddenly stepped into the imaginary circle they'd created and thrust his sword toward Sin. It was a move calculated to disrupt the monotony of their circular dance, rather than cause damage.

Sin reflexively did not move his feet, but leaned his chest and head back, out of reach of the sword. He straightened up as Hao pulled his weapon back.

Sin eyed Hao warily. His opponent was one year older than he was, giving Hao the advantage of a more mature, stronger, and more lithe body and musculature. He also was a head taller than Sin, and had a reach longer than Sin's.

Sin feinted his head and shoulders to the left, feinted right when Hao responded correctly, then swiftly stepped forward and swung his axe at Hao's shoulder. He missed his target as Hao dropped to one knee and then rolled away, before leaping back onto his feet.

This ballet continued. Sin thrust and missed. Hao thrust and missed. Sin parried Hao's strike with one of his own. Hao countered. They mirrored each other's moves, over and over again.

Two hours passed. Neither boy had landed a blow on the other, had as yet inflicted so much as a minor scratch or bruise on the other. Both boys remained mindful of the master's warning that if they both were alive when he returned in the morning, he would kill them both.

Hao moved in closer, his eyes locked on Sin's eyes, looking to detect the split-second before Sin might launch an attack.

Sin, had he been someone less well-trained than he was, would have tensed in response to Hao's move. Instead, he relaxed his muscles and set his legs in the traditional *Wing Chun* close combat, defense-parry Form, with his right leg directly behind his left leg, forming a straight line.

Hao spun and kicked at Sin with his left leg. Sin stepped back, out of reach of Hao's foot, then quickly stepped forward and spun around. He kicked Hao's left knee, dropping Hao to the ground. Hao balanced now on his uninjured right knee.

Hao pushed off and sprang to his feet, spun once again, then planted his right foot deep in Sin's midriff. Sin grunted and scurried away backwards to regroup, catch his breath, and regain his balance, as he stumbled to the ground.

Leaving no break in time between his kick to Sin's stomach and Sin's resultant grunt and retreat, Hao quickly advanced on Sin and thrust his short sword at him, missing him as Sin first rolled to his left, then sprang up, back onto his feet.

Sin swung his short axe, catching Hao just above his left hand, cleanly tearing through skin, muscle, and bone, as his weapon lopped-off Hao's hand at his wrist.

Hao jumped back, instinctively grabbing at his left wrist and raising it above his head to staunch the blood flow. He briefly looked down at his severed hand lying at his feet.

Hao swung his short sword in a wide arc, more to keep Sin at bay than to inflict damage to him.

Sin backed away to take his measure of his wounded brother.

Hao bled badly and would continue to do so unless he could

pause the combat and apply a tourniquet to his arm. Sin knew this, but had no intention of giving Hao that opportunity. He had not been trained to allow his enemies any respite in combat.

Sin stepped in close to Hao to keep the pressure on him, remaining just out of range of Hao's sword.

Hao's dagger laid on the ground, out of Sin's sight, still clutched by Hao's severed hand. Hao glanced over at his hand and dagger, trying to decide how to survive this ruinous situation.

Sin thought about the master's instructions. The sun would be up in a few hours and the master would return to the courtyard. He intended to be the only warrior alive when the master returned.

Sin continued to threaten Hao with his weapon, feigning attacks, forcing Hao to remain alert to defend himself, even as he inexorably weakened from his loss of blood. If all worked out as Sin expected, Hao would die sometime before dawn, before the master returned, fully bled-out from his wrist wound. If not, he would quickly kill Hao as the sun came up over the courtyard, finishing him before the master returned.

Sin looked at his adopted brother, his only friend ever, and thought, *This is good joss. What an auspicious way to begin my eleventh year in the Celestial Kingdom.*

He smiled.

CHAPTER 23

FTER ALINKA, AS NATALIA, HAD been suitably courted and then deflowered by Bing Wu-li, she and Wu-li continued to meet every six months when he traveled from Hong Kong to Shanghai for the occasion. They usually spent three days together before Wu-li returned home.

When she and Wu-li were not together, Alinka offered her services as an accomplished courtesan to other men, sharing with them all her skill as a flower-seller girl, and the pleasures of pillowing with her, but none of the affection she offered Wu-li. Both her beauty, grace, learning, and high intellect enabled Alinka to entertain only those wealthiest men in Shanghai she chose to spend time with.

On the third Sunday in May, as Wu-li prepared to leave Alinka for his usual six months' respite, he bowed from his waist, took her hand in his, and kissed her hand. He had never before said goodbye in this formal manner.

"You are very young, Natalia," he said, "and I am honored to have been your first, and now, special lover."

Alinka smiled, but remained silent, as called for by proper decorum.

"In spite of your age, you not only possess the conversation skills and the beauty of a high-class pillow woman, but also the ability to provide superb sexual services. I am honored to be your ongoing sponsor and lover. I look forward with great anticipation of joy to our time together again in six months."

Alinka, as ritual required, still said nothing. She lowered her eyes, bowed her head, and curtsied slightly.

With that, Wu-li turned, left the House of Fragrant Pleasures, and climbed into a rickshaw to take him to the train station for the more than twelve-hundred kilometers, and several days' trip, back to Hong Kong.

The rickshaw bounced along, with the coolie runner loudly cursing the cars, trucks, bicycles, pedestrians, and other rickshaws that failed to give way to his head-long rush to the train station. This was all part of the typical jostling, uncomfortable rickshaw experience — part of the raucous, grating, clanging and grinding-down noise of Shanghai, a condition the locals call *jenao*, a perpetual assault of the senses you either come to love or come to hate.

Wu-li and his rickshaw coolie were in sight of the train station when another rickshaw abruptly cut them off, causing Wu-li's runner to utter an exclamation and to jump as he let go of the two long poles he used to pull the cart, poles that had been tucked under his armpits and weighted-down by his frail body.

No longer constrained by the runner's slight body counterweight, the coolie runner's ends of the long poles suddenly shot upward toward the sky, causing the passenger portion of the rickshaw to abruptly drop to the ground under Wu-li's heavier, unopposed counter-weight.

The sudden downward drop of the passenger cart and its

abrupt crash against the roadway, propelled Wu-li upward and forward, ejecting him from his seat, throwing him past the front of the rickshaw. He landed against the cobblestone roadway, smashing the side of his head against the road, immediately followed by his full body weight, and its forward-rushing motion.

The momentum, his body's weight, and the unyielding, immovable surface of the cobblestone roadway combined to telescope Wu-li's spine into a small, crushed structure and to snap his neck. Wu-li was dead a few seconds after impact.

Alinka knew nothing of this mishap. She only knew that six months later, Wu-li did not appear for their appointed time together.

After several days passed without either Wu-li's appearance or a message from him, Alinka concluded that six months before she must have done something to offend Wu-li so that he'd had decided not to return to her. Her conclusion was reinforced when she recalled the anomalous ritual Wu-li had performed when he last said goodbye to her, kissing her hand and complimenting her skills, something he never had done before.

Alinka decided that this unusual farewell had not been his way of elevating her status as a courtesan, as she had originally, but wrongly thought, but that his formal way of saying goodbye had been Bing Wu-li's polite way of saying farewell to her.

CHAPTER 24

DECIDED TO KEEP MY GOODWILL visit to Eldest Brother as brief as possible, without offending him, so as to minimize the undercurrent of strain that always existed between us.

I entered the Heavenly Palace nightclub at approximately 3:00 p.m. Once I was inside, it could have been midnight in there. Like most such entertainment clubs, Eldest Brother's club did not have any windows or any clocks on the walls. Once you were inside, you had entered another world, one divorced from the reality of the outside world and time.

I knocked on Sun-yu's office door and entered when he responded. He smiled when he saw me.

"*Heya, — Hello*, Younger Brother, what a nice surprise to see you."

"I was nearby so I thought I would visit before returning to work," I said.

Eldest Brother beamed at this sign of respect I had just tendered to him.

"What has brought you to Frenchtown? A crime for you to investigate over here, away from your jurisdiction? Can you even do that, Younger Brother?"

"Actually, I may. Under the Police Forces Compact I now have jurisdiction in most of the territories and concessions.

But, no, to answer your question, not a crime over here, not this time. I came to Frenchtown to meet with Big-Eared Tu about two crimes that occurred in the Settlement."

I could see that Tu's name grabbed Sun-yu's attention. He sat up straighter.

"*Ayeeyah!* Tu?" he said, "I'm impressed. He actually met with you?"

I nodded. "He did, although he wasn't as helpful as I hoped. Still, since he did not express his opposition to my investigation, that was good *joss,* and made it worth having the meeting with him."

Sun-yu laughed. "I am not surprised he didn't oppose you. What crimes could you be investigating that could possibly interest a man as exalted as Tu?"

"The murders at two flower-seller houses — two murders — should have interested him. If there are more, eventually it will hurt his pocketbook."

Eldest Brother shook his head, smiled condescendingly, and made a clucking noise with his lips.

"Tu is a master businessman, Younger Brother. If he wasn't very interested, I am sure he had a good reason not to be, and that he knew what he was doing."

"Perhaps, but he said he dismissed my inquiry because he thought it didn't matter that a flower-seller girl and another's client were murdered. He said the victims were easily replaceable, and that soon, if not already, no one would miss their absences."

"Tu was correct, Sun-jin. Such people are easily replaced. You should not spend your time looking hard into such common crimes."

Eldest Brother's sentiment somewhat mirrored my

sentiment, yet I knew I had to solve these murders to please the chief inspector, or I would risk losing my job.

"So you say, Eldest Brother, but I don't judge which crimes are to be investigated or which are inevitable and therefore to be left alone. That is not my job."

"*Shi* — *Yes*, I know, and that is why you continue to arrest coolie women at the Baby Wall even though your superior officer then lets them walk free." He shook his head as if to say, *When will you learn?*

This was going nowhere. I didn't feel like being lectured by Sun-yu so I left him and returned to my office. So much for goodwill.

CHAPTER 25

ALINKA EVENTUALLY ACCEPTED THE OBVIOUS.
When three consecutive six-month periods passed without Bing Wu-li's reappearance in Shanghai, and without any message having come from him, she reluctantly acknowledged that he would not return to her. At first she was saddened, still convinced she had somehow offended him, and, consequently, had driven Wu-li away.

"That's not so, Natalia," Maggie File said to her on more than one occasion. "This has happened before with other flower-seller girls for reasons having nothing at all to do with mistakes made or offenses given by them. It is the way of men to enjoy a young woman, then to suddenly leave her to enjoy another, younger woman elsewhere."

Alinka was skeptical. "That does not describe Bing Wu-li," she said. "I must have done something wrong or he would not have forsaken me."

"If you had acted incorrectly," Maggie File said, "Bing Wu-li would have complained to me. That, too, is the way of sporting men. All of them. Since he did not complain, I can only conclude that his appetite for virginal young maidens over-powered his desire to be with you."

Alinka said, "Perhaps." But she did not really believe it.

Eventually, Alinka moved her memory of Wu-li from its conspicuous place in a front drawer of her mind, and instead stored it in the farthest-back corner of some remote back drawer. She now thought of Wu-li only on those rare occasions when something she otherwise experienced reminded her of him. Even then, she no longer grieved for his loss. She merely recalled him, and remembered that he had given her much pleasure.

Alinka kept her room at Maggie File's mansion and expanded it to incorporate the room next door. She now had a suite to use as her entertaining room. She carefully maintained her looks, and she cultivated and expanded her wit and conversation skills so that she entertained only the most wealthy clients, or men who, although not ordinarily rich, were temporarily flush from some gambling winnings.

Alinka welcomed her new client — a man named Lord Maxwell, an Englishman visiting Shanghai — to the House of Fragrant Pleasures. This was his second visit to the sporting house, but his first time with Alinka. He had recently seen Alinka escorting another client to her entertaining suite, and had inquired about her with Maggie File. He then arranged to take the formal next step required for a first pillowing experience with an exalted courtesan — he arranged to be introduced to Alinka (as Natalia) through the person of the woman he had pillowed with the night he first saw Alinka.

Soon thereafter, Alinka met with Maxwell over tea. After ascertaining that he was a member of British peerage, that he was cultivated, and that he was wealthy, she agreed to entertain him the following night.

That was when everything fell apart.

Alinka had barely slipped out of her camisole when Lord Maxwell grabbed her by her hair, wrapping its then-long strands among his fingers, and locking her hair in his tightly-closed fist. He yanked Alinka downward, forcing her onto her knees, as he continued to pull her hair.

When Alinka shrieked and tried to pull away, he slapped her twice, forcing her neck to recoil and strain.

Alinka spun away, then flawlessly slipped into her defensive *Kobudo* Form, protecting herself even as she sought an opening to attack.

She saw the opening.

Alinka stepped toward Maxwell, coming within one meter of him. She suddenly bent her legs, squatting, and, as she lowered herself, reached out and grabbed him between his legs, crushing his scrotum with lethal intent.

Maxwell screamed and doubled over, his hands buried between his legs.

Alinka slammed her palm into Maxwell's nose, flattening it, causing it to bleed in staccato bursts of bright-red, highly oxygenated blood.

Maxwell slowly rose to his feet, covered his nose with his palm, then quickly rushed over to Alinka.

As Alinka prepared to kick him between his legs, Maxwell reached into the pile of clothes he'd left on a nearby chair and pulled out a short-blade stiletto. He swiped the blade across Alinka's face, cutting her from just below her right ear, down her right cheek, to a point just under the edge of her chin.

Alinka screamed and dropped to the floor just as Maggie File, together with three large Chinese men she employed to keep order in the flower-seller house, crashed through the locked door. Maggie File carried a large, unsheathed carving knife with her.

Alinka slowly, but inexorably, recovered from her wound, but she never again was the same.

The stiletto cut required forty-seven, inexpertly-sewn stitches to repair it, and nine months to heal, during which time Alinka did not work. When finally she was able to work again, she had lost all her regular clients to the sporting house's other flower-seller girls.

"I'm sorry, Natalia," Maggie File said, "but those are the hard circumstances of our way of life." She shrugged slightly. "You had a good ride while it lasted, my dear. Now it's time for you to move on to a Number Two sporting house."

Alinka did not argue. She knew that what Maggie said was true. She had even expected it.

"I'll pack and be gone from here by the end of the week," Alinka said.

Maggie nodded her assent. No wealthy man wanted to pay for an expensive courtesan who looked as if she'd lost a knife fight.

Although Alinka's business as a courtesan had ended, her mind was fine and her bank account reasonably healthy, although it had been somewhat drained during the time she convalesced and was not working.

Over the course of the next three months, Alinka studied the art of cosmetics. She learned that through the careful application of makeup she could reduce the harsh appearance of her scar. Thus, although her face would not satisfy the rigid demands of the wealthy gentlemen who frequented the Number Three House of Fragrant Pleasures, her appearance, as well as her skills as a former courtesan, enabled her to work as a flower-seller girl — albeit one with unusual skills for a woman working at her now reduced rank — at a Number Two sporting house, this one located on Kiukiang Road in the French Concession.

The sporting house Alinka attached herself to — the Garden of Beautiful Pearls — was not one that would permanently damage her aspirations by attaching its own shabby condition to her reputation. The mansion that housed the sporting house was filled with Persian rugs, tasseled lamps, fabric on the walls, furniture covered with cloth, and a sparkling chandelier in the main parlor.

After nine months there, Alinka left the Garden of Beautiful Pearls. Using her dwindling savings, and a high-interest-rate loan made to her by Big-Eared Tu, Alinka rented an old mansion, hired six young flower-seller girls (including one thirteen-year-old who she would train to be courted and deflowered), several maids, a cook, a *shroff*, and one body guard. That done, Alinka opened her own licensed sporting house just off the Bund, on Nanking Road, behind the Customs House, as part of the Line.

Alinka called her establishment the House of Brilliant Jade. Her sporting house would be an upscale, Number Three sporting house.

CHAPTER 26

THE SUN HAD BEEN UP for one hour when the master returned to the courtyard.

As Sin heard the key turning in the lock of the courtyard door, he walked over to Hao's body and stood over it, his feet spread apart the width of his shoulders. He faced the door.

The master entered the courtyard, looked around, and absorbed the situation.

"Go into the house, my son, and clean yourself. I'll meet with you in the Great Room in thirty minutes. I will arrange to have this body," he said, canting his head toward Hao, "fed to the dogs."

———◆———

Sin sat on the floor in front of the master. He was wearing a clean white shirt and clean, white, long pants with an orange sash tied around his waist, the traditional garb of a *Wing Chun* fighter. He also wore an orange sweatband around his head. He had no weapon with him. The master sat cross-legged on a satin pillow facing him.

"You have done well in your first task, Chang Sin, my son. Now, as you are well within your eleventh year on this firmament, I have your first true assignment for you."

Sin seemingly remained impassive, but he silently smiled deep inside. He was excited, pleased, too, but also nervous. Now that he'd had his first kill, although the object of his success had been his friend and brother, he finally was fully blooded. He was ready to engage again, this time as his master's assassin.

"Yes, Master," Sin said. He bowed his head.

Sin felt his stomach tighten slightly at the suggestion he was ready to proceed on his own, unwatched, and not instructed by the master, no longer able to make the mistakes a beginner might make and still live to see another dawn. His apprehension, he realized, was not the trepidation of embarking on this new path. He felt ready to do so. His misgiving was that he might disappoint the master.

"You will find your way to the court of Warlord Tan Bey. You will kill him with poison at your first opportunity."

"Yes, Master, but how will I, a stranger, get close enough to the warlord to poison him? I am not a member of his clan."

"You will contrive a way to obtain a lowly position in his camp's kitchen. When you have been there long enough to have become familiar and, therefore, invisible to the warlord's guards, you will determine some manner in which to serve the warlord his food or his opium, which you will have previously mixed with lethal poison of some type.

"You have seven full moons to achieve your assignment. When you have done so, you will return to me. Not before."

The master paused, then said, "If you have not completed your assignment within seven full moons, do not return here to me. Ever. If you do, you will die."

CHAPTER 27

AFTER SUN-JIN LEFT BIG-EARED TU's home, Tu summoned Pock-Marked Huang to meet with him.

"I have just met with the inspector detective, Ling Sun-jin," he said to Huang. "He is with the SMP Special Branch. He is investigating the murders of a flower-seller girl and some client."

Huang seemed puzzled. He wrinkled his forehead.

"Why are you concerned, Master Tu? These killings mean nothing. Their occurrences are as routine as night following day. It is part of the business."

Tu extracted a cigarette from a fold in his gown, then waited for Huang to walk over and light it.

"You're sure of that, Huang? Would you stake your life on it?"

Pock-Marked Huang returned to his seat and fidgeted after he sat down. He looked at the floor briefly, then back up at Tu. "I believe it to be so, Master Tu."

Tu frowned. "That's not good enough. You have missed the point why I summoned you here."

Tu waited a beat for Huang to protest, to indicate that he understood why he had been summoned by Tu. When Huang remained silent, Tu said, "I should have known about these killings before they occurred, not afterward."

Tu's face flushed. He watched Huang squirm in his seat.

"I expect the opportunity to sanction them or forbid them before they occur. This was your failure, Huang." He banged his fist on the arm of his chair.

Huang said nothing. He stared at Tu and slightly bowed his head.

"You will find out who is behind these actions and report this information to me. I am treating these incidents as a first step by someone to challenge my authority, to wrench away my control of the opium trade. Someone willing to risk his head doing so."

"Perhaps they merely are crimes conceived of in stupidity, Master Tu, not meant to challenge you."

"You will determine that for me," Tu said. "Be sure of your information when you report it to me."

Tu paused to consider his next order to Huang. "And watch the policeman, too. You might learn much by following his investigation."

CHAPTER 28

WAS AWAKENED ABRUPTLY FROM A deep sleep by Bik dragging her coarse, pink tongue across my cheek in a warm dog-kiss. I opened my eyes in time to see her tail begin to whip back and forth as she realized I now was awake. I sat up in bed, put my feet on the cold floor, and patted her head. I then turned to Alinka, who was in bed behind me. I rubbed my eyes with the back of my hand and yawned.

Alinka was lying naked on her stomach, still asleep.

I left my bed to head to the commode down the hall. Bik stayed behind in the flat, drinking from her water bowl as I walked out into the common hallway.

When I returned to my bedroom, I realized I must not have been as quiet as I thought I'd been because Alinka was sitting up in bed, naked to her waist, but covered below with a light cotton blanket.

"Good morning, Sun-jin," she said, as she smiled at me.

"*Ayeeyah*, Alinka. Any morning I wake up and you are with me is a good morning," I said.

Alinka smiled again, then leaned back against the pillow, pulled aside the blanket that partially covered her, and opened her legs to invite me in.

I first met Alinka when I was visiting the Garden of Beautiful Pearls, a Number Two brothel located on Avenue du Roi, in an otherwise staid residential district in the French Concession.

My flower-seller girl companion for that evening — a comely White Russian woman who called herself Marta — and I had just climbed into bed when the sound of a piece of furniture smashing against the wall that separated our room from the entertaining room next door interrupted our proposed coupling. This was followed by shouts in English, as well as shrieking in a language I believed to be Russian.

When the commotion did not end — in fact, it seemed to be intensifying — Marta announced that she could not do her business with me with such a distraction going on. She insisted I go next door and have the people quiet down if I wanted to pillow with her that night.

"*Dui bu qi?* — *Excuse me?*" I said, astonished and annoyed by her demand. I wasn't sure I'd heard her right until I saw her fold her arms over her bare chest and cross her legs at her ankles. I understood the subtext of her message.

"*Ayeeyah*! I'm not going over there," I said. "Ignore them. I'll make you forget about them."

Marta remained adamant. I sighed, acknowledging that my night of pleasure would be ended before it even started if I did not resolve the ruckus next door. I put on my long pants, left the room in a foul mood, and headed next door.

No one answered my loud knock, but I must have gotten their attention because the noise abruptly stopped, followed by complete silence, as if they were listening for my next move. I banged again on the door, this time putting all of my policemen's authority into the stroke.

"The fuck you want?" someone — a male — with a commoner's British accent yelled. "Go away."

I knocked again, harder. "Open up," I said.

The door suddenly flew open and I faced an overweight man in his late thirties. His pale white chest was bare, his face crimson, and steadily growing darker as we stared at one another.

"What?" he said, using a tone that clearly displayed his anger. "Get lost before I crush your nuts." He glared at me with menace in his eyes.

"You need to quiet down," I said, speaking softly to set a good example. "You're disturbing other people."

"Who are you," he said, "a fuckin' constable or something?" He shook his head and spit on the floor next to my foot.

I nodded. My eyes hardened and lost the neutrality I'd been trained as a peace officer to bring to the opening of a potentially explosive situation.

Although I knew I had only limited jurisdiction in the French Concession under the Compact, I hoped he wouldn't know that.

"You've got it, my friend. I'm SMP, Special Branch, an inspector detective."

I reached for my warrant card ID before I remembered I was bare-chested and had left my ID in the other room on the dresser, along with my badge and pistol. I quickly dropped my hand to my side.

"You need to quiet down or leave," I said.

"Screw you," he said, and started to slam the door closed.

I placed my palm out and blocked the door from closing. Then I pushed back hard, forcing the door open all the way. I stepped into the entertaining room.

The room was a mess. A chair was overturned in one corner, and some other small piece of wooden furniture — I couldn't tell what it had been — lay smashed against the wall that was common to the entertaining room I'd just left. I assumed that this was the piece of furniture Marta and I had heard crashing against the wall a few minutes before.

A broken lamp lay by the bed. There was an empty liquor bottle lying on its side against one wall. A small rug was scrunched-up on the floor at the foot of the bed. The room smelled from spilled liquor, unbathed male, and the scent of a woman after sex.

I looked toward the bed and saw a mid-twenty-year old, naked, pale, Occidental woman crouching on the mattress. She held a large carving knife in her right hand. Her face had a look of defiance about it that made it clear to me she was determined to use the weapon if called upon to do so. I nodded at her, but did not approach her.

"What's going on?" I said to the woman, looking across the room at her, while I kept a wary eye on the man near me.

"*Vol!* — *Pig!* she said with a heavy Russian accent. "He paid for his time, got what he paid for, then insisted on going again for nothing."

She glared at the man, then turned back to me. "*Nyet* — *No.* I'm working. I don't give it away."

I turned toward the man. "Is that right? Did you get what you paid for?"

The man ignored me and glared at the woman.

"*Da* — *Yes,*" the woman said. "I told him we don't pillow again unless he first pays me again. I told the little piker we was done until then. That was when he started beating on me and throwing furniture."

"We're done when I say we're done, not before, Whore," the man said, looking over at the woman. His face had darkened again. He turned back to me with a scowl.

I looked hard at him, and said, "Get dressed and leave now."

"Fuck you," he said, as he took a step toward me. He made the mistake of grabbing my shoulder, then shoving me.

I reflexively slipped into the *Shaolin* defend-and-attack close-quarter Form.

I relaxed my legs and absorbed his next shove so that I did not fall away at all. I fisted my hands and sank down into a squatting position until my thighs were almost parallel to the floor. I held this position for three or four seconds, then emptied the weight from my left leg into my right leg, rooting my right foot. With all that completed in a matter of seconds, I rose up and spun quickly on my right leg. I kicked the man in his right knee with the inset of my left foot.

I refrained from kicking through the vertical plane of his knee because I didn't want to break his bone. I wanted him to be able to walk away from here so I would not have to call an ambulance, which would also cause the French Concession police to show up.

The man dropped to the floor with a shriek, holding his knee in both hands. Suddenly he turned to his left and reached over to his trousers hanging over the edge of a chair. When he brought his hand back around and again within my sight, I saw he was holding a small knife.

Playtime's ended. I thought. *Time to become assertive.*

I quickly spun and kicked him on the side of his head. He fell over, hitting his head on the floor. The knife skidded away from his hand. He was out cold.

"*Spasibo — Thank you*," the woman said. "Is he dead?" she asked from behind me, still kneeling in the bed.

"No, so you need to be gone from this room when he comes to."

"*Nyet*. I don't have nowhere to go tonight," she said. "I'm working. I have to be here."

I nodded. "I'm next door. Come in there if you want. The door will be unlocked." That was when I noticed the scar running from under her right ear, down her cheek, to just under the beginning of her chin.

"How did you get that?" I said, pointing at her scar so she would know what I was asking about.

"How do you think? From a lowlife like him," she said, pointing at the man on the floor. "Comes with the business."

I returned next door, and had just undressed and climbed back into bed with Marta when the door to our room opened. The woman from next door walked in.

She looked at me, then at Marta, then back at me.

I look at Marta, shrugged, then looked back at the White Russian woman.

I turned to Marta, and said, "Move over and make room. She's from next door." I motioned for the girl to join us in bed.

As she slipped in next to me, she said, "I am called Natalia."

When Marta left in the morning, Natalia stayed on.

And that was how I met Alinka Novikosha.

CHAPTER 29

E LEVEN-YEAR-OLD SIN HAD BEEN WATCHING the warlord's encampment for nine days, observing his armed guards, his personal staff, and his household staff. In that time, Sin observed a boy who seemed to be thirteen or fourteen years old, who came and went to and from the encampment with frequent regularity.

Sin covertly followed the boy on three occasions when he went into town, purchased kitchen supplies and foodstuffs, then returned to the encampment. On the boy's fourth trip to town, Sin arranged to be walking ahead of him toward town, on the path that would be traveled by the boy as he performed his errand.

As Sin heard the boy come up behind him, slowly riding the burro he'd ridden on each trip before, Sin turned back to face the oncoming boy, nodded his head at him as the boy came close, and said, speaking a crude form of the *Mindong* language spoken in Amoy, "May I walk to town alongside you? It will be safer for both of us if we do that?"

The boy agreed.

By the time the boy and Sin reached town and had spent

time together there as the boy completed his errand, the boy and Sin were as if old friends.

As the boy completed loading his burro with the packages he'd acquired, he said to Sin, "Where will you go from here?"

"Nowhere. I have no family, no ties. My only brother recently died. I have nowhere to go so I will wander the streets of the village, as a beggar, looking for work and food."

"Work?" the boy said. "If you want work, perhaps I can help you. Come with me to our kitchen. My cousin is the supervisor there. I am sure he will hire you to do something in the kitchen if you want."

And so Sin accompanied the boy back to the warlord's encampment where he met the boy's cousin. Sin was hired to help others tend to the livestock that the warlord's encampment bred and shuffled from camp-to-camp as it made its way throughout Fukien Provence.

After three months working in and around the livestock pen, and occasionally helping out in the kitchen between his livestock chores, Sin, who deliberately maintained a low profile, had become invisible to all but the livestock and the kitchen staff.

Sin walked to the nearest village where he sought out and entered the local herbal shop.

The dimly-lighted premises was typical of such stores, having a diversified inventory to serve all manner of customers. Bled-out chickens and other fowl hung from the ceiling, tied by long ropes so the customers could inspect their bodies before deciding to purchase them; fresh and decaying vegetables filled several bins; all manner of used clothing filled one rack;

and dusty, metal cans without labels or any other means of identification sat on shelves, promising to surprise anyone willing to purchase the cans at their discounted prices.

As Sin entered the store, he noted the location of the apothecary section toward the back. He wandered over.

As was customary, the visible portion of the apothecary stall was stocked with remedies of all sorts. There were several different types of antelope-horn powders to ward off old age; tiger-paw powder to make men more virile; other powders to eliminate headaches and other bodily troubles; herbs to make young women fertile; and, other herbs and powders to make middle aged and old women feel young again. There were roots to make skin glow, and others to clear-up pimples. There were herbs to make hair grow and others to make hair disappear. If you wanted it, the remedy was there just for the asking and for the right payment.

Sin walked over to the shopkeeper. "Good morning, Uncle," he said.

The man nodded. He looked warily at this very young stranger.

"I am looking for a special powder, something that will put an end to my enemies and will make those who would become my enemy think carefully about doing so."

"We have no such powders," the man said.

Sin removed five silver tael coins from his pocket and placed them on the unpainted, warped wooden plank that functioned as a countertop.

The clerk looked at the coins, then at Sin, then back at the coins. He reached out and smoothly scooped them up and placed the coins in a small leather bag that hung on a long cord draped around his neck.

"Come. We will go in the back."

Ten minutes later, Sin walked out of the store and back to the encampment, a small vile of white, tasteless and odorless poison-sumac powder hidden in his pocket.

Sin waited outside the tent for the boy whose task it was each evening to prepare the warlord's opium pipe, to fill the oil lamp that would be used to heat the pipe and vaporize the powder, and to cut and pulverize into a fine powder the small block of opium the warlord smoked each evening before retiring for the night with one of his concubines. The boy's name was Wang Pu.

"Wang Pu," Sin said to the boy as he emerged from the tent, "how goes it this night?"

Wang Pu looked up, surprised to be addressed by the live-stock boy from the kitchen. He didn't really know him though he'd seen him around the kitchen area and animal pens for several months. He nodded, leery of speaking with some boy he didn't know.

"Do I know you?"

"May I speak with you in private for a moment?" Sin said.

Wang Pu stiffened. *Was this some sort of subtle threat from this boy?*

"I have chores to do. I cannot be bothered talking right now."

Sin had anticipated this. He opened his palm and showed Wang Pu three silver coins — the equivalent of approximately seven months' salary for the boy.

At Sin's suggestion, he and Wang Pu walked behind the tent where they would be alone.

"I am requesting your help, my friend," Sin said. "I will reward you handsomely for doing so." He stared down at his hand to remind Wang Pu of its rich contents.

Wang Pu frowned and looked at Sin with a blend of curiosity, skepticism, concern, and greed.

"I don't know you. Why should I help you?"

"You have seen me in the encampment. I am on the staff of the kitchen master," Sin said. "I help tend the livestock and also sometimes work in the kitchen tent."

Wang Pu slowly nodded, but said nothing. He glanced briefly at Sin's open hand holding the coins.

"You'll help me because I will pay you more than half of one year's salary for you to do so," Sin said. He paused to let Wang Pu absorb this concept. He moved his open palm and the silver coins closer to Wang Pu.

"There will no danger for you in doing so, but your help will aid me in leaving the animal pens and kitchen staff, and obtaining some other, more glorious work here in the encampment. For that I always will be indebted to you."

The details were worked out, including the timing of the payment of the silver coins, with Wang Pu taking one coin immediately to whet his appetite for the others. He would receive the two remaining coins when he'd performed his task for Sin.

That evening, Sin and Wang Pu met half an hour before Wang Pu was required to deliver the ground opium and smoking paraphernalia to the warlord's tent. Sin made the balance of the payment to him when Wang Pu delivered the powdered opium, pipe, and oil lamp to him.

Sin retreated to his small tent where he mixed the white-powder opium with the white poison-sumac powder.

At the appointed time, Sin, accompanied by a watchful guard — who he'd convinced he was substituting this night for an ailing Wang Pu — entered the warlord's private tent and set up the opium delivery system.

Then Sin left the tent and secretly left the encampment.

The warlord, accompanied by a guard and his woman for the night, settled himself on the mat. He stretched out on his side. He placed the mouthpiece of the long pipe between his lips and held it there while he watched the guard light the oil lamp and place it under the part of the pipe that held the small cache of powdered opium.

As soon as the opium began to aerify, the warlord inhaled the vapors. Seconds later, he began to cough.

His lungs burned. He slammed his palm against his chest as he abruptly sat up. Breathing became more difficult as his lungs started to shut down, causing him to cough more frequently and more deeply.

The warlord wheezed and gasped for breath, as a drowning man would do as he periodically went under water and then briefly resurfaced again. He shook his head violently as if his motion could exorcize whatever was in his lungs, whatever was destroying his breathing, whatever was searing and blistering his internal tissue.

He tried to stand, but fell over onto his side. His cry for help emerged as a frog's raucous croak. He could not speak so anyone could understand him.

Bedlam reigned in the tent. No one knew what to do. A

CHAPTER 30

WAS SITTING AT MY DESK talking with another inspector detective when Chief Inspector Chapman summoned me to his office.

"There've been two more killings reported, Old Chap. One flower-

seller girl and her client."

I nodded. "Where did these occur, sir?"

"At the House of Brilliant Jade," the chief inspector said.

I was stunned. This dual crime immediately achieved an importance for me that the previous two murders had not. These murders had occurred at Alinka's sporting house. This meant that Alinka had been — and still might be — at risk of harm. With this one piece of information, the deaths in the Flowery Kingdom suddenly had become important and personal to me.

I left the station house and immediately went home to change into a nice suit of clothes, to pomade my hair, and to put a dish of water and some food outside my apartment building for Bik, since I didn't know how late, or if, I would return home tonight.

When I arrived at the House of Brilliant Jade, I asked to see Alinka. I was immediately taken to her.

"Are you all right?" I asked, as soon as I saw her.

"*Da*. I am fine, not the one hurt, but I worry this will cause my business to suffer."

We sat in a parlor on the first floor and shared a glass of *Baijium sorghum* spirits we both loved so much. We also smoked *Wang Yue Tai*-brand cigarettes. The atmosphere was tense.

"Tell me what happened," I said.

Alinka described how the cleaning-woman coolie had opened the door to Little Flowerbud's entertaining room and found two bodies on the floor.

"Did anybody see anyone enter or leave the entertaining room today?" I said.

"*Nyet.*"

"Did you know the client? Was he a regular? Someone who one of the girls might have had a problem with before?"

"Again, *nyet*," she said. "I did not know him. He was a new client. Today was his first time. I know all our clients." She nodded slowly several times, reaffirming her answer. Then she frowned.

I left Alinka and went to view Little Flowerbud's entertaining room. Fong, the photographer, and Dr. Yin, the criminalist, were there, finishing up their work.

I entered the entertaining room.

"Cause of deaths?" I said to Dr. Yin.

"Puffer fish poisoning. Both bodies show the external symptoms. Both vomited before they died and both had diarrhea. And this," he said, kneeling down and pointing to a small red mark on the woman's neck. "That's a puncture mark, likely a hypodermic-needle mark. The male also has one."

He stood up and continued. "The flower-seller girl and man also have distinct honeycombed patches on their skin. That's a typical symptom of the poison."

He lifted the flower-seller girl's robe to show me her thigh. I saw the honeycomb rash.

"Both victims must have suffered paralysis of their limbs, too," he said, "since their limbs are stiff. It's too soon for rigor mortis to have set in."

I nodded and made an entry in my notebook.

"And look at this," Yin said. "See how their skin has a slight blue tinge to it?" He pointed to the woman's cheek and left arm. "There's no evidence of choking or strangulation, so the color's from their diaphragms becoming paralyzed from the poison, shutting down their breathing."

"Okay," I said, nodding. "Anything else?"

"Only that they both were injected with the puffer fish venom. They didn't ingest it from a meal."

After Dr. Yin and Fong left, I studied the entertaining room and made notes of what I saw. I left the crime scene just as the transport team from the morgue arrived to remove the bodies.

I stopped by the kitchen on my way out to talk to the house cook.

"Has anybody else been made sick from puffer fish?" I said.

The coolie cook looked at me with confusion clearly written on his face. He replied just as I expected him to, but needed to actually hear from him for my report.

"We no serve puffer fish. Too much work to make safe."

I would confirm that with Alinka when I saw her, but for

now that statement was satisfactory. It also made sense in terms of the puncture marks found on both victims' necks.

I looked for Alinka before I left, but she'd already gone for the afternoon. She wouldn't return until near the dinner hour to prepare for that night's clientele.

As I walked out of the House of Brilliant Jade, I thought about Alinka. I was worried about her exposure to a killer, and planned to address that problem with her as soon as I could.

CHAPTER 31

WHEN ALINKA FIRST GOT TO know Sun-jin, after the night he had been with Marta, she assumed he was just another sporting man who was pleasant to talk to and pleasant to pillow with, but also one who, like many of the others she serviced, would come see her late at night when he had been lucky at a gambling parlor and had won a bundle of Shanghai silver. She was well-familiar with his type, and Sun-jin seemed to perfectly fit the pattern — reserved, distant, not very talkative, and very private, all traits Alinka actually welcomed in her clients.

After several of his visits, Alinka began to recognize something more in Sun-jin. What she had taken for indifference, for coldness, an absence of interest, she now saw as an internal stillness, a quietness that reflected a wariness with respect to life, a wariness that had made him seem cold and indifferent, but which was his internal skepticism born — she eventually would learn — from his experience in the streets of Shanghai as a policeman.

Once I'd met Alinka — she had finally told me her real name so that I stopped calling her Natalia — I visited her more than two dozen times to pillow with her. After my first few times with her, I noticed that as I dressed to leave her, she would say, "You come back to see me again, *Da?*"

At first I assumed she was just being an aggressive flower-seller girl who had found a reasonably sane and stable client, and wanted to encourage additional business from him. Gradually, however, I came to understand that she wanted me to come back to her because she enjoyed pillowing with and talking to me.

It had taken me much effort to come to terms with Alinka's business and what she did with other men in her entertaining room when we weren't together, but gradually I was able to put aside all thoughts of this. This was the first step in my realization that I wanted to be with her even when we were not engaged in business in her room, that I liked her as a woman, not just as a flower-seller girl.

Certainly, I liked her appearance — her short, dark, bobbed hair she wore in the style of a 1920s Hollywood flapper, and I liked her large dark eyes, full lips, tiny nose, and her sensuous body. But I also liked her mind, and was intrigued by her deep and diverse conversation. Alinka was my first experience dealing with a courtesan — even with a former courtesan — and understanding the difference between an exalted, trained Flowery Kingdom courtesan and an ordinary flower-seller girl, however beautiful and refined the flower-seller girl might be.

I had never known anyone who knew as many things as Alinka did. She spoke several languages, could correctly serve tea, knew about books, music, and art, and knew what went on in the secret minds of men and women — all matters that had always been beyond my reach and, the truth be told, beyond any interest I'd had until I came to know her better.

When Alinka talked to me of these things, I listened, and I enjoyed listening. She brought interest in many matters to me and awakened a side of me I hadn't experienced since my school days in San Francisco. I responded with many questions and, in time, with discussion, as I now read many books and learned more to keep up my side of our conversations.

The day came when I realized — and finally admitted to myself, but not yet to Alinka — that I liked her very much.

I liked the way she looked and the way she smelled. I liked the way she tasted during and after we made love. I liked the feel of her skin when I touched her, and the way she felt when I held her close to me.

I enjoyed the sound of her throaty, Russian-accented voice when she spoke, and the often-embarrassed giggle when she laughed. I liked the quiet stillness she wore like a cloak when she was merely silent, deep in thought, or was being sullen.

I liked, too, that I was comfortable telling her things about my work and about myself — things I'd never told anyone else and likely never would — and I liked, too, that I felt good telling her these things.

After I had known Alinka for about one year, I asked her to move into my flat and live with me. She said no.

CHAPTER 32

ALINKA WAS AT HER HOME in Big-Eared Tu's Happy Times Apartments thinking about several things she wanted to do later that day at the House of Brilliant Jade. Life in her sporting house finally was quieting down and returning to the way it had been before the puffer-fish murders.

It is good joss, Da! she thought, *that we are back to normal.* She laughed at the fact that she had just employed two concepts and two languages — Chinese and Russian — to make one point to herself.

Sin had been watching the door to Alinka's flat for more than one hour. He stood in an interior stairwell, looking through the small window in the door leading from the stairwell to Alinka's hallway.

It is too bad this woman does not want to live, will not fear death, that she will not care that I kill her, he thought, *because her loss of status as a courtesan has already brought her ultimate shame. This defective whore merely goes through the motions of being alive.*

He paused and smiled. *Killing her while she is away from her sporting house, in her own home, will strike fear in all flower-seller girls. They will know they are not safe anywhere, not even at home. This is as the master wants it, and will please him.*

Sin left the stairwell and walked to Alinka's flat. He put his ear to her door and listened. He heard nothing.

He pulled a light-weight balaclava from his pocket and placed it over his head and face. He removed his lock-picking tools from his other pocket and quickly lined up the pins in Alinka's door lock. He disengaged the lock, opened the door, and listened for Alinka's location, but heard nothing. He stepped inside and quietly closed the door.

Sin moved toward the kitchen and peeked around the edge of the open doorway. Alinka's back was to him, her hands submerged in dishwater in the sink.

He quietly stepped into the room and eased his way toward her. He pulled his double-wire garrote from his side pocket, and gripped an end with each hand, forming fists around the wooden handles. He spread his arms the width of Alinka's narrow shoulders, stretching the dual wires tight.

He took his final step toward Alinka, and prepared to loop the garrote wires over her head and down to her throat so he could pull the weapon tight and strangle her. He slowly lifted the garrote above Alinka's head.

Alinka sensed his presence. Or, perhaps, she heard something. She could not say which when later asked by the police.

Suddenly, without warning, Alinka dropped to the floor on one knee. In the same motion, she formed her fist and pounded it into the outside of her assailant's left knee, causing him to shriek from pain and drop to the floor.

Alinka sprang to her feet and dashed for the kitchen doorway.

As she passed him, Sin reached out and grabbed her by one ankle, yanked her backward, and brought her crashing to the kitchen floor. Alinka screamed in pain as her shoulder and right elbow broke her fall.

Sin rolled over, sat up, and then climbed on top of her, pinning her shoulders to the floor with his knees. He looked around for the garrote, but it was outside his reach. He balled up his right fist and smashed it into Alinka's mouth, then again, just above her left eye. He punched her once more — a third time — splitting her lower lip.

He leaned away to try to reach the garrote, but could not reach it without lessening the pressure on Alinka's shoulders. He was not willing to do that.

Sin placed his fingers around Alinka's throat, pressing his thumbs on both sides of center. *He would strangle this whore,* he decided, *with his bare hands.* He smiled at the thought of it.

Alinka strained for breath as Sin's fingers tightened around her throat. She became dizzy, began to lose consciousness. Soon, she stopped fighting her assailant and relaxed as she began to slip into darkness.

This will serve the bitch right for attacking my knee, Sin thought.

Sin heard a noise, the unmistakable sound of the flat's door opening and then closing.

"It's me, Missy. I'm here," Alinka's *Amah* shouted from the front room.

Sin froze in place and listened. He released his fingers from Alinka's neck, and slowly released the pressure from his knees, moving off her shoulders, as he started to quietly stand up.

Alinka remained in the dark, her eyes closed, her head lolled to one side.

Sin quickly moved behind the kitchen door, blocked from the *Amah*'s sight, and waited.

As the elderly woman entered the kitchen, rushing past the open door to Alinka, not noticing Sin who was behind the door, Sin slipped away and quietly left the Happy Times Apartments building.

CHAPTER 33

I WAS STUNNED WHEN I RECEIVED the call from Alinka's *Amah*, who was with Alinka at the Whangpoo Memorial Hospital on Kanting Road. She told me Alinka was there because she'd been attacked. I immediately left my office, caught a taxi, and rushed to the hospital to be with her.

Alinka definitely looked beaten-up. Her face was swollen and one eye blackened. Her lower lip was split and scabbed. She had black and blue marks on her forehead.

"He tried to choke me," she said, her voice thick and coarse, as she lifted her chin and pointed to the marks on her throat.

I leaned in and kissed her forehead. She winced. She was more tender than I'd expected.

Eventually, I was able to temporarily set aside my personal concern for her. I became an SMP cop again.

"Did you see who it was? Can you ID him?" I asked.

"He was Chinese," she said, "about one and one-half meters tall, and skinny, but strong."

"Did you see his face?"

"*Nyet.* It happened too quickly. He came at me from behind. I never saw his face because he wore a cloth mask." She looked away as if considering something to say next.

"I could smell him, though," she said. "He was Chinese." She paused as if reconsidering this. She shook her head.

"*Da.* He definitely was Chinese."

It was only later I learned that Alinka's *Amah* had saved her life.

I left the hospital and returned to my office. I deliberately avoided running into Chief Inspector Chapman by using the back staircase to get to my third floor desk. I did not want to pass by him on the way to my office because I did not want to have to lie to him, by deliberate omission of facts, not telling him I now had a personal interest in solving the Flowery Kingdom killings.

I settled in at my desk to think about my next move.

Everything had changed. I no longer resented having been assigned to the murder cases, not now that Alinka was in danger.

I realized that if Alinka was to remain safe, since she would not remove herself from danger by taking a holiday from her sporting house and moving in with me, I had to make her safe by investigating, then quickly solving, the crimes. This now became my primary goal. If I failed, Alinka might die.

CHAPTER 34

RETURNED TO MY INVESTIGATION. MY concern for Alinka's safety drove me forward.

I settled back at my desk to consider all the pending flower-seller girl cases. I mentally returned to the investigation by focusing on the classic techniques used by police to investigate crimes — paying attention to the crime scene, interviewing participants and witnesses, and learning about the victim's life and relationships (their friends, love relationships, enemies, criminal connections, criminal records, known bad habits, marriages, divorces, business conflicts, debts, and any other financial issues).

This sounds straight-forward, almost easy, but it isn't. Too much of this technique relies on the good faith participation (directly or indirectly) of people who are tangentially involved — the victims (whose bodies or histories might or might not yield valuable information), participants in the crime, and witnesses — all who need to be cooperative if they are going to be helpful to the investigation.

I also always find it necessary to remind myself, in the course of an investigation, to pay attention to the subliminal, ticking clock of the case, reminding myself that a case typically will be shut down by headquarters if too much time goes by without the investigator achieving meaningful results. This isn't because of nefarious interference by our bosses. It's a reflection of the reality of police work, of the economics of law enforcement. Resources, after all, are limited.

It is always necessary when I am investigating a particularly difficult case to remind myself not to fall into easy traps such as believing that sequence proves causality or that the facts are as I believe them to be merely because they support the preconceived dots that connect preconceived notions I might have about the crime.

When I finished running though all these considerations, as I reviewed my case files, I decided to return to the House of Brilliant Jade to again interview participants and witnesses. Although I had initially talked to everyone who seemed to be involved, I thought I should interview everyone again. I hoped that once the shock of the initial murders had worn off or lessened, someone might remember some small fact or detail they had not recalled before.

I knocked on the front door.

I hadn't talked to Alinka since yesterday, so I wondered if she'd been released from the hospital and had come back to work as she said she planned to do, or if she was still convalescing from her assault, notwithstanding her brave intention, as her doctor at the hospital wanted her to do. I would know in a few minutes.

The door opened and a house coolie allowed me to enter.

"Is Missy Natalia here?" I said.

"Missy not here."

That was good. Apparently, Alinka had shown good judgment and was continuing to convalesce as her doctor wanted her to. I asked to use a telephone, and called the hospital to confirm that Alinka still was a patient. She was.

I then asked to see the woman who had first entered the entertaining room belonging to the poisoned flower-seller girl and her client.

Her name was Shun Mei-ling. She had come to Shanghai from Soochow. She probably was seventeen or eighteen years old, but looked at least ten years older.

"Please sit," I said, nodding toward an empty fan-back, art deco-style chair.

I pulled up a three-legged stool and sat on it, facing her.

Mei-ling clasped her hands together and placed them on her lap, then sighed as if she had reached the final straw in this matter. She clearly was nervous.

The question I first had to resolve was whether she was nervous because she was about to be questioned by a policeman — a situation I encountered often — or if she was nervous because she had something to hide, something she feared my questioning might expose.

"Your name is Shun Mei-ling?" I said, speaking the *Hu* dialect.

"Yes, sir." She lowered her eyes.

"You were first to enter Little Flowerbud's entertaining room?"

She nodded.

"Did you know the client she entertained last night from other visits to you or to other girls here?"

She shook her head. "Never saw man before I pleasured him that night."

That caught me by surprise.

"You entertained that same man that night?" I said.

"Yes, sir. Before Little Flowerbud had her turn."

"Explain that."

Mei-ling described how the customer, when he arrived at the House of Brilliant Jade, had selected her from among several flower-seller girls who were lounging in the first-floor parlor.

She noted that the customer and she'd had sex — nothing unusual or exotic — and that she would have gladly pillowed with him again on some other night, based on their first encounter together, if he ever wanted her to do so again.

"After I pleasured the client, he said he wanted to pillow with some other woman he had seen in the hallway while walking with me to my entertaining room.

"When I finished cleaning myself and dressing, I took him to the first floor parlor where he pointed out Little Flowerbud as the woman he wanted to pillow with. I introduced them, then sat down to await the arrival of other clients."

"Okay," I said. "Did the man say anything to you to show he was worried he was in any danger?"

"No."

"Did Little Flowerbud?"

"No."

"Anything else you can think of that might be important?"

She shrugged. "I don't know what might be important."

I asked her to contact me if she remembered anything else. I didn't expect to hear from her.

The interview with Mei-ling frustrated me. I seemed to be getting nowhere fast, and Alinka's safety continued to weigh heavily on my mind. I still did not know what I was looking for, so I had to look at everything, absorb as much information as I could, and hope that at some point I would see some pattern emerge among the parts, some connecting relationships I clearly did not yet see.

This unfocused stage that marks the beginning of almost all investigations always frustrates me, although I know from experience that the decision concerning what is important and what is not from among all the pieces I was absorbing — the emergence of patterns — would come later, if at all. It certainly was too soon in my investigation for me to recognize any patterns.

I had lived through this procedure over and over again, yet this inevitable, unyielding process still annoys the Confucian in me.

In spite of all my years with the SMP, I have not yet learned to apply to the investigative process the important Taoist principle called *wei wu wei* — meaning, to allow things to happen on their own, without forcing them toward a result.

I now was in the stage of the investigation that called for *wei wu wei*, for looking, listening, asking questions, and absorbing information without trying to force what you learn into a preconceived theory of the case. This part of the investigatory process is invaluable, and it deserved its full due without being pressured by me because of my impatience. But, to be fair to myself, I have never been able to apply this principle to my life, in general, so why would I expect to be able to apply it to investigations I was involved in?

When Mei-ling left, I returned to the front parlor and asked the woman who seemed to be in charge in Alinka's absence if she had ever seen the victim-client before last night.

She shook her head. "No, officer, I have not."

I wasn't surprised or disappointed by her answer. I asked her to ask the same question of all the other flower-seller girls, and to tell their answers to Alinka when she came back to work. She said she would.

Before I left, I called the station house to see if any messages had come in for me. The officer at the front desk said that Eldest Brother had called, and that he'd said it was important that I call him back as soon as I received his message.

Instead of calling him, when I left the House of Brilliant Jade, I went directly to see Sun-yu at his club.

CHAPTER 35

WHEN I ARRIVED AT THE Heavenly Palace, Eldest Brother was in his office. I settled into a chair in front of his bamboo wooden desk. This time, we skipped the conventional Confucian preliminaries and dove right into the reason for our meeting. I could tell from Sun-yu's facial expression, as well as his abrupt speech pattern, that he was troubled by something.

"You called the station house to talk with me, Eldest Brother?" I said, using, on this occasion, the proper Confucian and Taoist salutation.

He nodded. "I'm instructing you to drop the investigation of the dead flower-seller girls and their customers," he said. "Do so immediately, Younger Brother."

I frowned. "I cannot do that. There have been too many deaths to be ignored. And now my friend, Natalia, is at risk.

"Besides," I added, "I do not have such authority at the SMP. You know that. But even if I did, I must see this through to its end unless I am ordered otherwise by my boss."

"Such an order can easily be arranged."

"Do not do that," I said, annoyed by the suggestion. "Such an act on your part would irreparably damage us."

Sun-yu shook his head and turned-up his eyeballs so only

the whites of his eyes showed, giving me what we Chinese call *giving someone White Eyes*. It is the traditional Chinese physical statement intended to show contempt for another person or for something that person had just done or said.

"If you need to make an arrest, Sun-jin, to satisfy your conscience or to appease your superiors, an appropriate person will be made available to you, and the required evidence also will be available. This can easily be arranged, but you must cease your investigation."

My back stiffened. I shot a hard look at Sun-yu that should have knocked him off his chair and onto the floor, but, in reality, didn't faze him.

"Don't ever say that to me, Sun-yu. Understand."

"Your actions are offending people we cannot afford to offend. It is neither wise nor safe for you to proceed with your investigation. We both will suffer if you do not back off."

"*Ayeeyah!* Who put you up to this?" I said, my voice growing more shrill as I spoke. "Big-Eared Tu? Pock-Marked Huang? Some other criminal you want to curry favor with?"

"That is no concern of yours, Younger Brother. Your concern should be the nature of the message, not the identity of its author. Your concern should be to end the investigation while you have time to do so."

I could feel my neck and head growing hot.

"And it is no concern of yours either, Sun-yu," I said, "how or if I do my job." I opened and closed my fist over and over again.

Sun-yu stood up, saying nothing in response to my statement. He turned away and walked out of his office. I sat and waited. I was curious to see if he would come back. I decided to give him ten minutes, then leave.

When he returned a few minutes later, he was carrying two empty glasses and an opened bottle of Tiger Wine, that foul-smelling drink made from tiger bones that have marinated and disintegrated in rice wine. Unlike Occidentals who generally find Tiger Wine disgusting, Sun-yu and I love the beverage.

Eldest Brother poured drinks for us.

"Drink up," he said. "Then let's start this talk over as if we haven't yet spoken."

He swallowed his drink in one quick gulp. Then, before we could start over, as he'd suggested we do, he slammed his empty glass down on his desktop with such force I involuntarily jumped in my seat.

Eldest Brother apparently had already forgotten we were supposed to start this conversation over, without our accumulated rancor.

"You must stop your investigation immediately," he said again, a large measure of strain now infecting his tone.

"This is not a request, Sun-jin. I am ordering you to do so as my younger brother." He stared at me and shook his head once as if he was fed up with my continued lack of appropriate sibling respect.

I said nothing. I was trapped between my ambiguous, legacy-driven, Confucian sense of family duty and my Confucian-fueled obligation to follow the rules and continue to investigate the crimes. And, of course, I also was driven by my concern for Alinka's safety.

Eldest Brother and I stared at each other without speaking for what seemed forever. Finally, he broke our deadlock.

"Please, Sun-jin," he said, trying to recover the tone of our conversation as it had been when I first entered his office, "please do as I say, as I ask. If you do not, you will be endangering yourself and others you care about."

"Like who?" I asked, although I thought I knew the answer.

"Like you and me, like your friend, Natalia, and also my wife and five children."

"Who passed this message to you to deliver to me?" I asked again.

"That is of no importance to you. What is important is that you heed the warning. It will not be given again."

"That's not good enough, Sun-yu," I said.

"*Ayeeyah!*" His tone became strident again. "It is essential you do as I say, and I say you are to immediately stop your investigation. Do you understand me, Younger Brother?"

I understood all right, but I was not going to comply, at least not while Alinka might still be in danger, although, as Eldest Brother suggested, she might now be in danger merely because I was continuing my investigation.

CHAPTER 36

SIN PREPARED HIMSELF FOR HIS next assignment — an assassination to take place at a Japanese sporting house in Hongkew.

———◆———

Hongkew is the area of Shanghai, north of where Soochow Creek and the Whangpoo River converge, in the section of the city that used to be in the treaty-port area formerly known as the American Settlement. Hongkew became part of a larger district, the International Settlement, when the Americans and British merged their treaty territories.

The district is heavily populated by Japanese, who both live and work there. The Hongkew Japanese (as well as the home government in Tokyo) treat Hongkew as a protectorate of Japan even though it is part of the International Settlement. Its residents and governing council enforce Hongkew's arbitrary protectorate status.

The Japanese in Hongkew maintain special sporting houses that are licensed by local Japanese authorities, sporting houses that employ Chinese, Korean, and Japanese women. The sporting houses are maintained according to a strict code of health regulations enforced by local Japanese authorities. The houses service all nationalities.

Twenty-one-year-old Sin had been fulfilling assignments for the master for ten years now, and was well-skilled in selecting the weapons he would use, the ways in which he could infiltrate the environment of a target, and his means to complete the kill, then escape. He was a seasoned, professional assassin.

Sin's weapons of choice continued to be the ancient weapons he'd been trained with when Hao was alive. To that small inventory, he had added the venom of the much coveted puffer fish.

Sin dressed in a night-soil collector's outfit, and entered the House of the Ascending Sun, a Number Two sporting house, through the back door service entrance.

He looked and acted as if he had business to perform there. He carried a large, empty wooden bucket in one hand, and used a walking stick for balance to confirm that he was an old man — as he had disguised himself to appear to be. He spoke with the madam, who approached him as he made his way toward the interior of the mansion. Sin spoke with a faux, elderly-type voice.

"You are here to be pleasured, Uncle?" the woman said. "You did not need to enter through the back door."

"I am here to remove the honey pots from the third floor commode," Sin said.

"You are making your rounds early tonight, Uncle. Is there some reason for that?"

"I am making my rounds based on what the Number One Boy told me to do when I was here last night. I don't ask questions. I just do what I'm told."

"Very well," the woman said. "Get on with your work, then remove yourself through the back door. Be quick about it and do not disturb our flower-seller girls or their clients."

Sin nodded, then climbed the staircase to the third floor.

The hallway was empty. Sin glanced at his wrist watch. Two a.m.

He stood in the hall, near the door to the commode, and listened. Sounds emanated from behind several closed doors up and down the hallway.

Taking his cloth bag with him as cover, if needed, Sin put his ear to one door and listened. Someone moved about inside, but he did not hear voices. *Perhaps*, he thought, *the person in the room is alone.*

He slowly turned the door's handle, and prepared to step into the room. If confronted by more than one person, he would feign ignorance and confusion, saying he was an old man and was lost, that he was looking for the commode.

The room was dark.

Sin closed the door behind himself and stood still, letting his eyes adjust to the gloom.

A flower-seller girl, alone in her bed, seemed to be asleep.

As he left the entertaining room, Sin thought, *Strangling the woman had occurred so easily and quickly, much more easily than I anticipated.* He nodded and smiled. *I should find another target.*

The hallway was still empty.

He decided to repeat the crime in another entertaining room. He put his ear to the door next to the room he'd just left.

As Sin quietly let himself out the back door of the sporting house, he smiled. *The master will be pleased,* he thought.

He had performed his assignment tonight many times over. Never before had he slain seven victims in one evening.

Yes, he thought as he slipped away from the sporting house, *the master will be pleased.*

CHAPTER 37

ALINKA WAS HOME FROM THE hospital. It now was more than two weeks since she and I spent the night together. Various factors had interfered, including the assault upon her in her home. All week now, each time I visited her at her flat, the assault on her, and my fierce desire to protect her, stood as silent barriers between us.

I decided we needed to flush this out. I did not want these problems to continue to grow until they became insurmountable for us.

"I'm worried about you," I said.

"*Nyet.* Don't be. I'm fine."

"I don't think you are, not since you were attacked."

I could see Alinka's posture become a little more rigid, her eyes narrow, and the corners of her mouth slightly turn down. I braced myself.

I took a deep breath before I said what next needed saying, for what I had to say was bound to cause more tension between us.

"I think the attack was meant for me," I said, "not for you, intended to send me a message, a warning." I paused a beat, then added, "I'm sorry for that, Alinka."

I didn't really believe this, although Eldest Brother had

predicted it, and it might have been possible. But if so, if the attack was a warning to me for having ignored Eldest Brother's order to drop my investigation, then the person who ordered the attack on Alinka had no idea what would motivate me or what would dissuade me. Threatening the woman I loved would only spur me on to catch them, not deter me. But I did not want to explain that to Alinka, and hoped she wouldn't raise the point.

Alinka studied me for a moment. I couldn't tell how she was processing what I'd said, not until she finally spoke.

"Why do you say that, Sun-jin? You were never mentioned during the attack. Perhaps you are too close to this matter to view it objectively."

I decided I had no choice other than to tell her the truth, although I worried it might frighten her.

"Because I've been told to back-off the investigation or risk having people I care about harmed."

Alinka slightly shrugged. "If that's so, then, *Nyet*. I'm not going to stop living my life because some people have issued vague warnings to you. I've worked too hard to regain what I now have to step away and lose it again."

I shook my head. "But that's my point. Your work carries inherent danger with it. Why add to that by continuing to work right now? Take a rest period until the crimes are solved and the killer arrested or put down."

I took a deep, calming breath and briefly held it before making my next statement.

"Take some time off," I said. "Come live at my flat until this is over."

Alinka's face reddened. "*Nyet*, Sun-jin, I will not compromise my life because of veiled threats. I'm disappointed you would ask me to do so." She shook her head sharply as if to underscore her statement.

"Besides, Sun-jin, you are being a hypocrite. You know you do not approve of the House of Brilliant Jade, and you are using this investigation and the attack on me as the first step in having me leave my business.

"You do this even though you make use of flower-seller girls from other sporting houses. I am not blind to your actions, and I am not naive."

"No—" I started to say, but stopped as I watched her frown. She'd pretty much figured me out on this point.

I definitely would have liked Alinka to leave the business, even though, as far as I knew, she no longer serviced customers. I dropped the subject, walked over to her, and kissed her forehead. It was like kissing a slab of marble.

CHAPTER 38

BIG-EARED TU WAITED UNTIL THE last warlord and Pock-Marked Huang had taken their seats on silk, embroidered cushions on the floor of his Great Room. He had summoned them to him to give vent to his anger and to spur them on to solve the problem he increasingly believed amounted to the beginning of a plot to overthrow him as the ultimate authority in Shanghai's underworld.

"The police are becoming a nuisance," Tu said, looking directly at Huang as he said this. "The inspector detective investigating the sporting house murders has not made sufficient progress to enlighten us as to their true origin and purpose, yet his efforts hinder our own efforts by removing evidence we otherwise would control. That is not acceptable."

"I will deal with the policeman, if you wish, Master Tu. Just instruct me to do so," Huang said.

"Not yet," Tu said. He waited a beat, then said, "Continue to watch the policeman, Huang." He looked over at the warlords and nodded once.

"I intend to instruct the Council to terminate the investigation. We will see what the policeman does when he no longer is sanctioned to investigate.

"Based on what I've learned about this inspector detective,

I expect he will continue to investigate the murders in spite of orders otherwise.

"His actions might be enlightening. Perhaps he will lead us to the person who wants to supplant me as leader of the Green Gang."

Tu looked at Huang the whole time he said this.

CHAPTER 39

WAS SITTING AT MY DESK reviewing the files I'd created for the Flowery Kingdom murder cases.

I keep two types of files: files of current investigations I am working on — updating them from time-to-time as I learn new information or come up with new ideas or theories — and secret files I keep on the non-public personal and business habits of Shanghai's prominent citizens, placing into those files information I come across as I investigate various crimes.

With respect to this latter group of files, only I know I have them. I store these files at home, in the back of a closet in my flat. They exist for a rainy day should I ever need them.

As for the case files, I am pretty much alone among all the inspector detectives at the SMP who believes in and keeps detailed files of cases.

We all keep copies of the official reports from the criminalists, of course, and we all keep copies of the reports from the morgue. We also all keep copies of the official photographs made at the crime scenes. This much is mandated by SMP procedures. But I am pretty much alone in keeping detailed summaries of my interviews with witnesses, as well as elaborate notes about my theories of the cases as I work through them and as they evolve and change.

I also try to keep my notes and summaries short, concise, and to the point so any other inspector detective can read them and fully understand my thinking about the cases. But no one has ever asked me to show them my case files.

"The chief inspector wants to see you, Inspector Detective," the sergeant-major said.

Now what? I wondered.

"Seven flower-seller girls were killed last night at one sporting house," the chief inspector said.

I frowned. "Seven?"

"And this time — not just because of the number of girls murdered, although that plays a role — the case is even more sensitive than the others you're working on. It must be handled with the utmost discretion and care," he said, "and wrapped-up quickly and quietly."

"Yes, sir. Of course."

"The killings occurred at a sporting house in Hongkew."

That surprised me. Not that the murders had occurred in the Japanese protectorate, that was no surprise, although crimes of violence were rare in Hongkew. What surprised me was that we were going to be involved in investigating the murders there because, for the most part, by reason of convention, power struggles, and convenience, Hongkew was considered off-limits to the Settlement's SMP Special Branch, even under the terms of the Compact.

"Hongkew?" I said, as if I hadn't heard him correctly.

"Hongkew," he said again.

The Japanese in Hongkew maintain their own police force, consisting of about two hundred-fifty men. It is called the *Nihon Ryohi Keisatsu* — the Japanese Consular Police. While formally a division of the SMP, the JCP acts autonomously, and rarely calls upon, or accepts help from, non-Japanese police officers working for the SMP. We have almost no working relationship I know about with the JCP.

"Sir," I said again, "did I hear you right? Why would we investigate murders there? I doubt we'd be welcome by the JCP or be of much use to them."

"You heard me right, Inspector Detective."

"But, sir, can we even be effective there? Interviewing witnesses, I mean." I wasn't sure I wanted to know his answer because it couldn't possibly lead to anything good for me.

The chief inspector didn't answer. Instead, he looked through the contents of a file sitting on his desk. I continued to stand in front of his desk for a full minute before he spoke again.

"The murders of the seven sing-song girls occurred in the House of the Ascending Sun. It's located at the intersection of Luna and Dragon Roads," he said.

I noticed that on this occasion he used the British term for flower-seller girl — sing-song girl — rather than our local slang, flower-seller girl. I also noticed he hadn't answered my question.

"The commissioner of police, our consul, and the Japanese consul have agreed that the time has come to end these killings before they begin to affect business for all concerned, or affect Generalissimo Chiang's struggle against the Communists in Shanghai.

"We've been ordered to cooperate with the JCP to solve these murders. The JCP has received like instructions to cooperate with us," he said.

I knew this was not going to end well for me.

"So, Inspector Detective," he said, looking hard at me, "you will go to Hongkew, meet with the JCP inspector detective running the case, and you will aid him in his investigation and cooperate with him in all respects. Understand?"

"Yes, sir."

The chief inspector narrowed his eyes. "You will set aside your petty Chinese prejudices against the Japanese, and will assist him in every way possible. Do you understand?" he said again.

"If I might say something, sir, isn't the real question whether the Dwarf Bandit running the investigation will cooperate with me? You know how insular and locked-down Little Tokyo is, and how prejudiced the Dwarf Bandits are against we Chinese."

"You will cooperate with him, as ordered, Inspector Detective, or you will face the consequences back here from me. And stop using that derogatory, Chinese phrase when referring to the Japanese. I don't care for it."

"Yes, sir," I said. I hadn't expected him to answer my question, and he did not disappoint.

CHAPTER 40

I RODE THE ELECTRIC STREETCAR FROM headquarters to the far end of the Bund, then walked through the Public Garden toward the Garden Bridge.

As I walked leisurely through the park, thinking about how I would deal with the Dwarf Bandit in charge of the Hongkew investigation, and considered various possible scenarios once he and I met, I was stopped on two occasions by Caucasian British SMP constables who were patrolling the park. They wanted to know what I was doing in the Public Garden, and both times required that I show them my warrant card ID to justify my presence there, reminding me, as if I didn't already know, that as a general rule, neither dogs nor Chinese were permitted in the park.

I soon reached the end of the Public Garden and walked across the Garden Bridge into Hongkew.

As I stepped off the bridge, the world changed.

My first sight was that of the three-story-high Hongkew Market. This massive structure took up a full block, sprawling north from the Whangpoo River. There you could buy, at all hours of the day and night, poultry, fruits, fish, meat, and, if you were a Dwarf Bandit, Japanese female companions.

I continued north past hole-in-the-wall stores, Japanese

silk factories, pawn shops, medicine and herb stalls, hotels, and restaurants of every sort. Storekeepers and merchants stood at street corners and cried out for my attention, offering me silks, Asahi beer, Japanese china, cherries and other fruit, fish, and cotton kimonos, among other wares.

I walked past the expensive Broadway Mansions Apartments — the newest luxury apartment house in Shanghai, opened earlier this year.

Soon I came to the corner of Luna and Dragon Roads, the site of the House of the Ascending Sun.

A young Japanese woman, dressed in a kimono, admitted me, then led me to an entertaining room on the second floor. As I entered, I noted the presence of a woman who seemed to be in her late fifties — the sporting house madam, I assumed — and a man who seemed to be in his mid-forties. The man was dressed all in black, in an ill-fitting wool suit. He barely looked up at me as I entered, and did not greet or acknowledge me.

I stepped over to him, walked up to his face, and said, "SMP Special Branch Inspector Detective Ling Sun-jin here." Then I took a step back to give him breathing room. I showed him my warrant card ID.

The man grunted something under his breath that I couldn't quite hear, and wouldn't have understood had I heard it more clearly, since he'd spoken Japanese.

"And you are who?" I said, expecting to be treated to the courtesy of seeing his official credentials. He didn't answer. I mentally cataloged that information for future use.

He seemed to be a typical Japanese in Shanghai, thinking and acting as if he was superior to we Chinese, to the British, and to the Americans.

The Dwarf Bandit stood a little more than 1.8 meters tall. He weighed, I would guess, less than 57kg. He was clean shaven except for facial hair above his upper lip, the common decor of the Japanese in Shanghai.

The man reached inside his suit-jacket pocket and pulled out his billfold. He showed me his warrant card ID. I had no idea if it was an official JCP warrant card ID or not since I cannot read Japanese. I also was not able to see the SMP seal on the card since he closed his billfold so quickly.

"I am Inspector Detective Akio Harue," he said, speaking in heavily accented Mandarin. "I am in charge of this investigation. You will obey me in all respects and take orders from me." He punctuated his statement with one sharp nod of his head.

"I'm here to cooperate with you, not to take your orders," I said, also speaking Mandarin. "I understand you are under instructions to cooperate with me."

Harue frowned as I said this. His dark, bushy eyebrows briefly melded together into one thick, dark caterpillar.

"You will leave the House of the Ascending Sun now," he said. He stomped his foot once. "You are not welcome here. You will not participate in this investigation until you agree to submit to my authority."

With that, Harue turned toward the woman standing across the room and said something to her, speaking Japanese.

The woman bowed to him from her waist, turned toward me, and said in passable Shanghainese *Hu*, "You will come with me. Now."

I followed the woman to the front door, did not return her cursory head bow, and left the building as she slammed the door behind me.

CHAPTER 41

ALINKA ENTERED HER OFFICE ON the fourth floor of the House of Brilliant Jade, locked the door behind her, and removed the receiver from the telephone sitting on her second-hand banker's desk. She did not want to be interrupted. She needed undisturbed time to think through the recent events that had affected her personally — the attack on her in her flat — and those that had affected her business — the two puffer-fish murders at her sporting house.

Although she never would admit it to Sun-jin, she was worried about her personal well-being and about the impact on her business of the recent crimes in the Flowery Kingdom. She had so much to lose after all her hard work to rebuild her life.

Was she a specific target or a target of opportunity? she wondered.

Had she been attacked as a message to Sun-jin, as he had said, using her as a warning to him to back off his investigation?

Was the assailant someone who worked for her or was it someone who was related to one of her employees?

Frustrated by her inability to unearth answers from the fragmented, sparse information available to her, Alinka decided she had no choice but to conduct her personal life and her business as if none of the adverse events had occurred. But she also decided that she should do so with a wary eye, looking out for any signs of trouble.

CHAPTER 42

AFTER I DESCRIBED TO CHIEF Inspector Chapman what had occurred with Inspector Detective Harue, he chewed me out for not having agreed on the spot to permit Harue to run the investigation and to order me about.

"I thought I was clear with you," the chief inspector said. "You are not in charge of the investigation at the House of the Ascending Sun. What part of what I told you before wasn't clear, Old Boy?"

I had no answer for that. I didn't think, however, that it would be prudent of me to remind the chief inspector just now that he'd told me that my relationship with Harue was intended to be mutually cooperative. I shook my head in silent surrender to circumstances and to the chief inspector's authority.

"You were clear, sir. It was the Nipponese who provoked me with his arrogant, superior attitude. Like all Dwarf Bandits in Shanghai," I gratuitously added.

The chief inspector brushed aside my excuse with a wave of his hand.

"I don't care how he acts, Inspector Detective. You are under my orders. I gave you a command before. You will follow it."

"Yes, sir."

"When we finish here, you will contact the JCP inspector

detective and arrange to meet with him again. And this time, Old Chap, you will conduct yourself correctly or you will be back walking a beat again."

"Yes, sir."

"You will forget about your foolish, Chinese notions of face, and you will suitably apologize to the JCP officer when you see him again. That's an order." He paused, then added, "Am I clear?"

"You are, sir."

"When I next speak with you, Inspector Detective, I expect your report to be that you and the JCP inspector detective are working in harmony to solve this case. Do you understand me this time?"

"I do, Chief Inspector."

Apparently I wasn't the only one who had received a dressing down from his superior officer. When I telephoned Inspector Detective Harue to arrange to meet with him again, he seemed a different man. He showed some warmth and some interest in my participation in his investigation. We agreed to meet the next morning at the House of the Ascending Sun.

CHAPTER 43

Pock-Marked Huang stood in front of Big-Eared Tu, and waited to be offered a seat. He'd been summoned to Tu's home.

Tu did not offer Huang the opportunity to sit. Instead, he extracted a cigarette from an inner pocket hidden in his gown, placed it in the corner of his mouth, then nodded to Huang, signaling his former boss that he wanted him to light his cigarette.

When Huang completed this act of submission, he returned to his standing position before Tu, and waited for his boss to initiate the conversation.

"The Municipal Council will soon end the investigation. It is scheduled to meet in two nights. The decision will be made then," Tu said. "Meanwhile, the JCP and SMP have agreed to cooperate to solve the seven murders at the House of the Ascending Sun in Hongkew."

Huang nodded. He shifted his weight from one foot to the other, and back again.

"You will contact the Nipponese who is running the investigation and explain to him why, notwithstanding his orders from the JCP, he will not cooperate with the SMP or its inspector detective. Do not tell him the Council will soon be shutting down the SMP's investigation."

CHAPTER 44

AFTER SUN-JIN HAD LEFT THE crime scene in Hongkew that first time in response to his abrupt dismissal by JCP Inspector Detective Harue, but before Sun-jin and he had their telephone call resetting their meeting, Harue thought about the brief, distasteful meeting he'd had with the Chinese inspector detective.

He was a pompous fool, Harue thought, *like all Chinese policemen. Too full of himself. He should know better than to resist orders from a JCP inspector detective.*

He should understand that the Settlement and French Concession parts of this city remain unoccupied by us only by the good grace of the Emperor. Unoccupied for now.

Harue watched as the photographer took his photographs and the criminalist made all his measurements, searched the seven entertaining rooms for fingerprints, and collected dust. When the technicians finished, Harue examined the crime scenes himself, taking notes as he did so. When he finished, he released the crime scenes to the morgue attendants, and watched as they bagged the seven flower-seller girls, and removed the bodies from their entertaining rooms for carriage to the Hongkew morgue.

Everyone on the scene concurred. The girls had been

garroted, except for two who had been strangled by hand. It was obvious from the double-wire cuts or fingermarks on their throats. The only question was, who did this, and why?

Harue finished up, then released the seven entertaining rooms to the house's madam for cleaning and her further use.

As we had arranged in our telephone call, I met again with JCP Inspector Detective Akio Harue. Whatever goodwill — genuine or mandated — that existed during our telephone call setting up our meeting, it had ended sometime after our call and before I arrived at the House of the Ascending Sun.

"You now understand you take orders from me?" Harue said, as I came into his presence.

I thought about losing my job and my inspector detective's warrant card ID, so I nodded. "I understand."

Unlike the last time we met, when Harue wore an ill-fitting black woolen suit, today he wore a less severe, but still ill-fitting double-breasted tan suit. I suppose that was his nod to the recently arrived heat and humidity.

Harue also had a long saber hooked to his belt on his left side, a custom followed by every Shanghainese JCP officer I'd ever met. And, unlike those SMP cops who were not members of the Special Branch, and, therefore, not permitted to carry firearms except with specific permission in each instance or for special occasions, Harue sported a large pistol holstered on his right hip. It seemed to be a 20mm Nambu Taisho 14 Shiki pistol, but I wasn't certain. I had only seen this weapon in catalogs, never before in real life.

The Dwarf Bandit looked like a little man playing dress-up soldier or cop.

"I would like to see the seven crime scenes," I said.

"Crime scenes all studied by criminalist and then photographed. Since then, all cleaned up by house coolies," he said, speaking crude Mandarin.

He smiled. "Seven rooms put in condition for use by other sing-song girls after I finished. Nothing to see there anymore."

That did not please me. *How can I properly investigate seven homicides when I cannot examine the crime scenes? You don't release a crime scene until far along in the investigation. You never know what might turn up later, elsewhere, to send you back to look at the scene again.*

I thought about my specific orders from the chief inspector. I took a deep, calming breath.

"In that case, I would like to see the reports and photographs."

"Not ready," Harue said. "When ready, you apply for pass to come to Hongkew station house to see them." He bowed slightly. "You call me. I will help you get pass in spirit of cooperation."

A vision of me walking a beat as a constable flashed across my mind. I held my tongue.

"I'd like to speak with the flower-seller girls, if more than one, who found the victims, then with the house's madam," I said. I was quickly running out of credible requests.

"I already talk with them. You can read my report when it is ready. You wait until you get pass and then come to station house. Sing-song girls and madam have work to do. Cannot waste time repeating stories."

I was about to remind Harue that he was supposed to cooperate with me in the investigation, not to be placing obstacles in my way.

I opened my mouth, said, "Listen, Harue—" then abruptly stepped toward him, prepared to chew him out for not cooperating with me. But then I remembered the chief inspector's admonition not to anger the Dwarf Bandit. As before, the vision of me walking a beat in a constable's uniform flashed through my mind. I sighed.

I stepped away and looked hard at Harue, then said in the most obsequious Confucian manner I could conjure up, "Thank you, Inspector Detective Harue. I look forward to reading your report and to examining the photographs at your station house. All at your convenience, of course." Then I reluctantly, but prudently, shut up and left the premises.

CHAPTER 45

SIX WARLORDS AND POCK-MARKED HUANG gathered in Tu's Great Room.

"The Council will soon shut down the SMP's investigation of the sporting house murders," Tu said. "The inspector detective will be ordered to move on to other crimes and to ignore the Flowery Kingdom cases."

There was general agreement among the murmurs that this was a good thing.

"The JCP, however, refuses to cooperate with the Settlement's Council. It insists on continuing to investigate the murders that occurred in the House of the Ascending Sun."

There was general agreement again, this time acknowledging that the Japanese in Shanghai needed to be taught their place in Chinese society.

"Huang," Tu said, as he locked eyes with Pock-Marked Huang, "you will continue to keep the SMP policeman under close observation. Our information is that the Council's order, when it comes, is more likely to fuel his desire to solve these crimes than it is to stop him.

"I expect him to approach the JCP, too, so he can gather information from their continuing investigation. I have given orders that they are not to cooperate with the SMP policeman if he contacts them."

CHAPTER 46

THE NEXT MORNING, AFTER I fed Bik and let her loose outside, I thought about a plan I had conceived as I laid awake the night before, unable to sleep. I would visit the House of the Ascending Sun again and interview the flower-seller girls.

I knew that what I was about to do violated the order from Chief Inspector Chapman that I not visit the sporting house without the prior consent of Inspector Detective Harue. I didn't care. I was being shut out of the investigation by Harue, and would not sit still for that, not while Alinka possibly remained in danger.

I was prepared to give up my career as an SMP inspector detective, if necessary (but was not ready to walk a beat again as a constable) to protect Alinka, and so would resign from the SMP if it came to that. But I would not be dismissed from the investigation by Harue, as I clearly had been.

The woman who answered the door when I knocked at the House of the Ascending Sun was not happy to see me. I practically had to force my way into the mansion.

I wasn't sure what I could accomplish by this visit since

the crime scenes had been released by Harue, and they likely now were compromised by further use. Perhaps, at best, I could show Harue by my presence there against his wishes that he could not so easily dismiss me. I wasn't sure what that would accomplish other than to cause me to feel good, but feeling good in this circumstance had its own value.

I asked to speak to all the flower-seller girls who had found the seven bodies.

"They not here." The woman bowed her head slightly.

I asked to see the entertaining rooms where the crimes had been committed. I hoped that something might have been missed before the crime scenes were released back to the sporting house, and were thereafter contaminated. I was told they all were in use at the moment and would be occupied all day.

I said I would like to talk to any of the sporting house's other employees who had been working the night when the murders occurred. The woman said she would first have to telephone Harue and get his permission.

That was my cue to leave, so I did, first telling the woman not to bother Harue, that he was too busy to be disturbed by such a trivial matter. I did not want to give him the satisfaction of knowing he had beaten me again.

CHAPTER 47

A S I TOOK MY SEAT in front of the chief inspector's desk, I swear I could see steam coming from his ears.

"What were you thinking, Sun-jin? I gave you a direct order to stay away from the Hongkew sporting house unless Harue was with you."

"Yes, sir," I said.

"Harue's threatening to go over my head and file a complaint with our Council and with the commanding officer of the SMP — my boss. You know what that will do to our careers."

I nodded.

"Harue also said that if he learns you've gone back to the sporting house again without him being along, he'll personally come to the Settlement to arrest you."

I shrugged slightly.

"He also said," the chief inspector added, "that if he sees you anywhere at all in Hongkew, he'll shoot you on sight."

The chief inspector paused and smiled. "I believe him, so I'm considering ordering you to go for a slow walk through Hongkew to see if he's bluffing."

"I understand, Chief Inspector," I said. I didn't think this was funny at all.

The chief inspector shook his head and sighed. "Seriously, Sun-jin, what am I going to do about you?"

I didn't think he really wanted me to answer that, so I said nothing.

"You're confined to your desk for thirty days. You'll be doing paperwork until you can complete forms with your eyes closed.

"I'd suspend or fire you," he said, "but you're still benefiting from the Distinguished Conduct Medal you received, although I don't know why after all this time. So you get one more chance. But just one. Understand?"

"Yes, sir. I understand. Thank you."

I cast out my most humble look and sniffled once for effect. "May I ask a favor, sir?"

"A favor?" He paused as if to make sure he'd heard me correctly. "You're kidding, right?"

"No, sir, I'm not. I would like you to post a guard at the home and at the sporting house of my friend, Alinka Novikosha, until the killer is caught. She's already been attacked in her home, as you know."

The chief inspector shook his head. "Sorry, Old Chap, but we don't have the resources. She'll have to fend for herself."

In that case, I thought, *I can't drop the investigation just because I'm assigned to desk duty. I'll investigate at night, on my own time, and wrap this up before Alinka is harmed.*

CHAPTER 48

Chief Inspector Chapman was uneasy. He'd met with Lord Bingham only once before, that time being when the Honorable Lord had interviewed him on behalf of the Municipal Council for his present position with the SMP. The experience had not been a pleasant one for the chief inspector.

In addition to knowing at that time that his career with the SMP would rise or fall based on the interview, Chapman had been made even more uncomfortable because the meeting had taken place at the Shanghai Club, a premises normally off-limits to the likes of him — employees and prospective employees of the SMP.

Yet here I am again, he thought, *three years later*, as he approached the massive white marble building, summoned there by Lord Bingham to meet with him at this hour to discuss some subject as yet unknown to him.

Chapman walked up the marble steps, passing between two fluted Ionic columns as he did so, then walked stiffly through entrance doors held open by a tall, full-bearded Sikh, who was dressed in a spotless white uniform, with an orange turban on his head.

He entered the main hall with its twelve-meter-high ceiling. He glanced across the room at the ornate doors of the twin elevators that connected all floors, and at the long, curving white-marble staircase that ascended to the next level.

Although the chief inspector had not been given a courtesy tour of the building on his only previous visit there, he knew a great deal about the club and its structure from accounts that had appeared from time-to-time in the *North China Daily News* as background for other stories.

He thought about that previous visit as he entered the building. He would have loved to have seen the upper floors, with their specialty rooms, and, of course, to have seen the fabled Long Bar.

But that would not occur, he thought, *not ever. Not unless a murder is committed up there, and I run the investigation as a pretext to snoop, as I would, of course.* He silently chuckled at his private joke.

Such a tour, in the ordinary course of things, would be too commonplace for any member of the club to conduct, especially for someone as important as the Honorable Lord Bingham.

His thoughts were interrupted when another tall Sikh walked up to him.

"May I help you, sir?" he said, as he blocked the chief inspector so he could not move further into the lobby without the consent of his questioner.

"I have an appointment with Lord Bingham. My name is Chief Inspector Chapman."

"Yes, sir, his Lordship is expecting you. Please follow me."

Chapman had hoped that this time he would be led to the Long Bar where he would stand alongside Lord Bingham and discuss the reason he had been summoned. Instead, he was taken to a private room just off the lobby's entrance.

The Sikh knocked twice, then opened the door, although

his knock had not been answered. Chapman and his escort entered the room and stopped just inside the door.

Lord Bingham was alone, sitting in a Queen Anne wingback chair, reading a newspaper. He had a cigar in one hand and the folded paper in the other. A cocktail of some sort sat on a small table to his right.

The Sikh and Chapman stood waiting, silently.

After almost a full minute had passed, Lord Bingham put aside the paper, drew on his cigar, then expelled the smoke. He took a sip of his drink. Then he slowly looked up at his visitors, as if he were just noticing them.

"You may leave us alone now, Wafa," he said to the Sikh.

"Yes, your Lordship," the Sikh said, as he bowed slightly. He turned away, left the room, and softly closed the door.

"Be seated, Chief Inspector," Lord Bingham said, as he nodded to a smaller, slightly lower-to-the-floor chair to his front left.

He offered the chief inspector neither a drink nor a cigar as he proceeded to consume the two he'd been working on when the chief inspector entered the room.

Lord Bingham pulled hard on his cigar, stared briefly at the gray ash he'd created, then looked up and said, "Do you like your job, Chief Inspector?"

Chapman was puzzled and taken aback. *What had he done wrong?*

"Yes, Lord Bingham. I most certainly do."

He wondered if he should ask what he might have done to offend his Lordship or the Council, but decided to remain quiet, to see where this would go. He expected he would learn that answer soon enough.

"Good," Bingham said, his flat, dead eyes not matching the

optimism of his statement, "then this shouldn't be a problem since I assume you will want to keep your present position."

"Of course, Your Lordship. What shouldn't be a problem, sir?"

Bingham took a sip of his drink, then placed it back on the table. He stared at the glass for a beat, then again looked up at the chief inspector. He narrowed his eyes.

"What I am about to instruct you," he said, "shouldn't be a problem, Chief Inspector, not if you wish to keep your job."

Chapman was confused, but sat silently, waiting for some statement from Bingham that would clarify the Lordship's statement for him. He could feel his dress shirt sticking to his back, and a pool of perspiration forming in his armpits and on his chest beneath his dress uniform jacket.

"I have an instruction for you on behalf of the Council," Bingham said.

"Yes, sir." Chapman's back stiffened. This could not be good news under the circumstances of its delivery. His lower back began to ache.

"You will immediately cease all investigations involving the murders of sing-song girls or their clients," Bingham said.

The chief inspector was confused. *How could this be? This certainly was not the message he'd received from the Council after the occurrence of the first murder.*

"May I ask why, Your Lordship?"

"No, you may not." He drew on his cigar again, then again studied the resulting ash on its tip.

"But—"

Lord Bingham cut him off. "May I remind you, Chief Inspector, you work for the Council, at our pleasure."

Chapman nodded. "Yes, sir."

"And may I further remind you, Chief Inspector, you just indicated you like your job and would want to keep it. Need I say more?"

CHAPTER 49

IT WAS IN THE EIGHTH DAY of my thirty-day desk-bound suspension, completing some routine forms and other paperwork, when the sergeant- major walked over. This was becoming a frequent occurrence, although I wondered how my desk-bound status could affect anything the chief inspector might have in mind for me if, as I assumed I would soon learn, the chief inspector wanted to see me in his office.

"The chief inspector wants to see you," the sergeant-major said. The sergeant-major gave no reason for the summons when I asked him if he knew why.

When I entered the chief inspector's office I was told to close the door. I was not offered the opportunity to sit. The chief inspector remained seated behind his desk. He seemed pensive.

"When your desk assignment ends, Old Boy," the chief inspector finally said, "you will not resume your investigation into the Flowery Kingdom murders."

I was dumbfounded. "Why, sir? You said before that the Council was anxious to—"

"I know what I said before, Inspector Detective. That was then. This is now."

"But, sir—"

"This is an order directly from the Council," he said, "not from me. I wasn't told why."

"But we have nine flower-seller girls and two clients dead, at last count, sir. We have no reason to think these crimes will stop if we drop the cases now."

This was the worst possible news as far as I was concerned. It meant Alinka would remain at risk without any hope that the criminal or criminals would be caught.

"I know, Sun-jin, I know, but orders are orders, and we will follow them."

"But—"

"No *buts*. I was ordered to end the investigation, and now I'm ordering you to do so. This is not optional for either of us. You won't continue to work on it again, not even from your desk while you are on desk duty, or on your free time at night, as I expect you plan to do."

"Yes, sir."

"Once again I have to ask you, therefore, do you like your job, Sun-jin?"

"Sir?" I felt my spine involuntarily shiver.

"Follow my order this time or you will be sacked. That's my promise to you, Inspector Detective. No more warnings."

CHAPTER 50

A s the sun lowered in the sky, casting long shadows, I walked along the Bund, parallel to the river.

I walked past the gleaming white marble façade of the Shanghai Club, past the Customs House with its famous clock tower, past, too, the North China Daily News Building, the Sassoon House, the Shanghai Chartered Bank, and past Jardine, Matheson & Company's headquarters.

As I came to the Hong Kong & Shanghai Bank building with its golden dome, I walked up the steps to its entrance, which is flanked on both sides by two large, bronze lions. Although normally I scorn superstition, on this occasion I followed the tradition that most people observe as they enter and leave the building — I touched one of the beasts, hoping that doing so would give me good *joss*. I'd decided I could use some good luck right now.

I needed this time out of the office, time away from my desk, to think about what the chief inspector had ordered me to do — or, more like it, ordered me not to do — and to think about the cases I no longer was permitted to investigate.

I had no immediate answers to the questions swirling around in my head.

My immediate concern was to come up with some way to

protect Alinka since the SMP would not provide protection for her and I would not be out there looking for whoever might want to harm her.

I walked to Frenchtown. I could see the luxurious Broadway Mansions Apartments in the distance as I crossed the Garden Bridge. I walked further on and saw the Happy Times Apartments, Alinka's home. I turned west and walked along Avenue Joffre until I came back to the river. Then I crossed the Garden Bridge again and headed home. My head was no more clear now than it had been when I started my stroll.

As I neared my apartment building, I heard a loud buzzing tone in the street as a barber pounded his tuning fork — the barber's *huan tou* — announcing his arrival in the neighborhood so anyone who needed a haircut or shave would know to come outside. I nodded at him as I walked by and watched him as he put down his small, triangle-shaped, wooden bench he carried with him as he waited for customers to take a seat on it.

I didn't see Bik waiting outside the front door, so I entered the building and climbed the stairs to my second floor flat.

I thought about why Chief Inspector Chapman and the Council were so anxious to end my investigation. It was counter-intuitive.

Was I getting too close to something I shouldn't see and know?

I didn't know the *why* of all this, but I did know this much: as in all matters of the chain-of-command, the chief inspector obeyed his superior; his superior obeyed the Municipal Council; and, the Council obeyed . . . *Who?*

I paused. I nodded several times. *Maybe the answer to that question would be where I would find the solution to my investigation.*

I thought about the implication of that.

I intended to find out.

If I could do that much, I might identify the person *who* was blocking my investigation, and, in doing so, also find out *why* they were blocking it. That, I expected, would eventually lead me to the killer.

CHAPTER 51

ELDEST BROTHER CALLED THIS MORNING as I finished practicing my *Shaolin* Form. He said he would like to stop by my flat before I left for work. That caught my attention. It both alerted me to a possible problem and made me curious. Eldest Brother hadn't been to my home since he and his wife visited me here the first week I moved in three years ago.

I told him, of course, he was welcome to stop by, but I also said I was curious about the reason for his visit. He said he would tell me when we were together, that he had some important information to discuss with me, but did not want to talk about it over the telephone.

Sun-yu arrived one hour later. He laughed when he saw Bik, asked me how long I'd had her, and said he was surprised I would take the trouble to care for a dog.

"If you tire of her, Younger Brother, my kids would love to have her."

"I won't tire of her," I said. "More likely, she'll tire of me and run off at some point. She's a wild dog."

We settled into my living room.

"I recently talked with Big-Eared Tu," Sun-yu said. "He sent you a message."

That puzzled me. If Tu had a message for me — and I had

no doubt he did based on what Sun-yu just said — I would have expected him to summon me into his presence so he could deliver it in person. Tu did not have a reputation either for being shy or for using cut-outs to deliver his messages and make his points. Tu's mere presence when he delivered a message himself would inherently carry unbounded, coercive weight for the listener, including for me.

"Why would he send me a message through you?" I said.

"I had occasion to meet with him recently. He probably assumed we would soon be seeing one another. Or, maybe, the message for you was Tu's way of telling me to visit you. Either way, here I am with his message."

I didn't accept that explanation at all. "What's the message?"

"Big-Eared Tu said you should listen to your employer."

"Anything else?"

"No."

"What's that mean?"

Eldest Brother shrugged and said nothing. He looked at me expectedly, as if I would know what Tu meant, and would tell him.

"Did he say I should listen to my employer and should cease investigating the murders at the Flowery Kingdom?"

I didn't give any thought to how Tu might have learned about the chief inspector's order to me to stop my investigation. After all, Tu knew everything important that went on in Shanghai. Why wouldn't he know this? He likely had eyes and ears within the SMP.

"No, not specifically. He just said you should listen to your employer," Sun-yu said. I assumed that meant you should end your investigation, as you told me you've been ordered to do anyway. Just like I told you to do."

I thought about that. *Not necessarily.*

"Tu's message was subtly worded, Sun-jin," Eldest Brother said. "He was indirectly threatening you should you not heed his instruction to stop your investigation. You need to listen to him."

"What were his exact words?"

Sun-yu thought about my question, then said, "His exact words were that *you should pay attention to your employer.* Same as what I just said to you."

Not quite. "Tu was not threatening me, Eldest Brother. There are other possible meanings in his statement."

"Of course he was threatening you. Why else would he send such a mysterious message to you? Big-Eared Tu is not a man who makes idle statements."

"I don't believe it was an idle statement," I said, "but I also don't believe it was a threat or warning." I paused a beat.

"I think I know what he meant," I said, "and I'm satisfied his statement was neither a threat nor a warning to me."

I thought about the irony of this situation. Eldest Brother, the flexible Taoist, was acting like a rigid Confucian, seeing only a threat or warning in Tu's statement because Tu was a master criminal. He was not seeing layered meanings, other possibilities in the statement.

I, on the other hand, who often was justifiably accused of being a rigid Confucian, now took the Taoist approach and saw several possible meanings in Tu's statement.

I didn't bother passing this observation on to Sun-yu. The irony of it would have been lost on him — and that, in itself, also was ironic, given his Taoist temperament.

Once I'd settled at my desk back at the station house, I decided to concentrate on Big-Eared Tu's message to me.

I did not take Tu's words as an implied threat that I would be harmed if I did not cease the investigation. Based on my most recent meeting with him on this matter, I didn't think he cared, one way or the other, if I proceeded with my inquiries or not.

I thought about his exact words. I wanted to discover the possible meanings in their many layers.

The key words, as far as I was concerned, were that I should *pay attention* to my employer. While that could mean that I *should listen* to the chief inspector and end my investigation, I didn't think that was Tu's intent. After all, if it had been, Tu could have just said that I should stop investigating the crimes. In that case, I would have stopped. I was not a suicidal fool.

I thought the cryptic phrase might have meant that I should *watch, heed, be mindful of,* or *be careful of* my employer — the SMP, or, perhaps, just the chief inspector, my immediate superior officer.

Why would he say that to me? I wondered. *What was the statement's hidden message? Was it a friendly warning that my superiors at the SMP were not on my side when it came to the investigation, that I should be wary of them?*

That interpretation certainly would be consistent with the order that came from the Council pulling me off the case, I thought, *closing down my investigation.*

But who on the Council would give such an order to the chief inspector, and why? After all, the homicides still were unresolved.

Answering those questions, I decided, would be my next goal.

CHAPTER 52

S IN SAT ON THE FLOOR with his legs folded under him, contemplating the assignment just given him by the master.

He had been ordered to kill five flower-seller girls or madams or their clients in five days — one each day, all to be performed within the next week, each one to occur in a different Number Three sporting house.

Sin smiled as he thought about the master's concluding words: *The mere number of deaths in so short a time in five upscale sporting houses will instill fear within the world of the Flowery Kingdom.*

Sin decided he would use each of his five favorite antique weapons for this assignment — one for each kill.

First, he would use the bow and arrow — called, in Shanghainese, the *Gongjan* — to kill the target from a long distance. This would make everyone wonder how vulnerable they might be when they entered or left a sporting house.

For the second kill, he would use the short-handle axe — the *Foutou* — to kill, and then to behead, his next target, as a way to remind people he could be cruel as well as efficient.

Next, for kill number three, he would use the short sword — the *Yuchangjin*.

For his fourth kill, he would use his poison-tipped curved

dagger, which he will have dipped in the bacteria-laced intestine of the puffer fish.

Finally, for the fifth kill, for the madam who had survived his attack in her home because her *Amah* had interrupted them, he would use the double-wire garrote so he could enjoy watching her assist in her own death.

CHAPTER 53

S IN PREPARED HIS WEAPON FOR the first kill.

He selected two long-bow arrows from among several he'd recently constructed, and placed them on the floor next to him. The arrowheads were made from copper that Sin had sharpened to razor-like deadliness. The shaft of each arrow was made from flexible, but strong, young bamboo. The fletching of each arrow had been plucked from mature eagles specifically bred to provide feathers for arrows.

Sin's bow was his pride and joy among all his ancient weapons. The bow was a Qing Dynasty long-bow constructed from antelope horn, wood, and sinew. The weapon was medium size, as long bows go — 1.9 meters — with prominent string bridges. The bow had been designed to sacrifice arrow speed in favor of stability and the ability of the archer to efficiently and quickly launch long arrows that were up to 1 meter in length. It was the perfect long-distance, silent weapon for a trained assassin.

Sin sat up in a tree in a blind he'd constructed the night before, just after 3:00 a.m. He had, at that time, intuitively measured the distance from the blind to the front door of the sporting house at fifty-five meters. An easy shot for him on a day, like this day, without wind.

The sporting house was the House of Multiple Joys. He had already performed one assignment there, his first killing in the Flowery Kingdom, and had considered not returning there again for this assignment. The master, however, had emphasized that the five killings were designed to terrorize the flower-seller girls, the madams, and their clients, so he wanted Sin to perform his five hits in houses considered upscale and safe, all Number Three houses along the Line, that were visited by prominent and important men and women.

Sin did not have a particular target in mind at the House of Multiple Joys, so long as his victim wasn't the house's madam. One madam — the woman who would be his fifth kill in this assignment — would be enough to satisfy the master. He didn't care if his victim was a flower-seller girl or one of her clients. His goal was to create a sense of vulnerability in the people he did not kill, both at the chosen sporting house and elsewhere, by impaling his victim as he or she walked out of the sporting house.

<hr>

The sun had been up for just over three hours. Sin, in that time, had barely moved. He was the perfect, disciplined sniper.

At a few minutes past 9:00 a.m., a chauffeur-driven, dark green, 1934 Marmon Sixteen convertible automobile pulled to the curb opposite the entrance to the House of Multiple Joys. The vehicle's driver, a Celestial Being, honked the automobile's horn in three short blasts to signal the car's owner that his vehicle had arrived.

Sin set an arrow in the bow, and watched the porch door. He

pulled the bowstring tight until the arrow's fletching touched his right ear. He sighted the doorway along the bamboo shaft, then relaxed the bow's tension and waited for his target to step out onto the wrap-around porch.

After ten minutes passed, the driver turned off the car's engine, climbed out of the vehicle, and began to slowly polish the driver's side front fender with a cloth he'd extracted from his back, pants pocket.

Another fifteen minutes passed. Suddenly, the sporting house's front door opened and a man, dressed in black evening wear, stepped outside. He hesitated briefly, as if surprised to see bright daylight, then started walking across the broad porch toward the steps leading down to the sidewalk, heading toward the automobile. The chauffeur stood at attention, his right hand on the top of the rear passenger-door he'd opened when he saw his approaching passenger.

As the man took his first stride off the porch onto the top step, Sin sent his arrow flying toward him.

Seconds after its release, the arrow slammed into the man's chest, just at the top of his heart, knocking the man off his feet and backward toward the porch. He was dead before he hit the wooden planks.

CHAPTER 54

SIN COMPLETED KILLS TWO AND three without incident. The fourth kill proved more interesting.

For each kill, Sin had disguised himself as a cleaning coolie, and easily gained entrance to the three sporting houses through their back entrances used by tradesmen and service workers.

Sin used his short-handle axe for kill number two. When he left the entertaining room, he took the dead flower-seller girl's head with him, carrying it in a trash sack he casually draped over his shoulder. He left the decapitated body in plain sight in the entertaining room.

Sin performed kill number three with clock-like efficiency. He dispatched the flower-seller girl while she was using the bidet, down the hallway, away from her client and her entertaining room. For this task, he ran his short-handle sword blade, tipped with puffer fish poison, through her heart.

For his fourth kill, Sin actually performed cleaning-coolie duties on the third floor of the mansion, using a broom he'd brought with him to repeatedly sweep the hallway. No one noticed him — not the flower-seller girls, not their clients — as they came to and went from the entertaining rooms. He was an invisible service coolie.

Sin watched as a middle-aged white man left an entertaining room, followed by a flower-seller girl a few seconds later. She said goodbye to her client, then turned away as she tightened the sash on her satin robe, and walked down the hallway toward the common commode. She brushed past Sin as she walked, forcing him to stop sweeping and step aside. The flower-seller girl ignored him.

As soon as the woman closed the door to the commode, Sin entered her empty entertaining room. He waited for the woman to return, standing by the wall, where he would be hidden by the opened door when the woman entered her room.

The flower-seller girl opened the door and stepped into her entertaining room, untying and shedding her robe in one swift, practiced motion, as she came through the doorway. She reflexively closed the door behind her without looking back, and stepped toward the mirror on the far wall to retrieve her entertaining outfit from a nearby hook.

As she took her first step toward the mirror, Sin reached out from behind the closed door and grabbed the woman's neck from behind. He pulled the woman into the center of the entertaining room, keeping her off-balance by dragging her backwards.

The flower-seller girl twisted her body, even as she fought to gain purchase on the wooden floor. Unable to break free, she suddenly went limp as she saw the face of her assailant, his arm raised to slash her throat with a curved-bladed knife he held in one hand.

The woman instinctively stomped her foot hard on Sin's

ankle, just at the point where the top of his foot and ankle met. Her wooden sandal tore Sin's skin and bruised his bone.

Sin involuntarily cried out, then cursed loudly, instinctively letting go of the woman in the same desperate breath.

As the woman sprinted toward the door, Sin grabbed her by her hair and yanked her off her feet, back toward him. Without wasting any more time, Sin cut the woman's throat.

CHAPTER 55

M Y MANDATED INACTIVITY — MY exile to my desk as punishment — left me cranky and restless. I was engulfed in a sense of worthlessness. After all, I was an inspector detective. I should have been out in the field trying to solve other crimes, even if I now was prohibited from investigating the murders at the sporting houses. There was a sufficient inventory of other crimes that could benefit from my experience.

Instead, I was spending my days reviewing files and reports, looking into various minor robberies and other second-rate crimes that had occurred, but had not been solved, and so now were on hold, making sure the files were in order. It was no comfort to me that the chief inspector, when he gave me this mindless assignment, had said that this duty was perfect for me because I kept the best files of any policeman he'd ever known.

I spent my nights after work watching the Baby Drawer, hoping to save male infants, but not making any arrests because even this activity probably was a violation of my punishment and could get me into deeper trouble with the chief inspector. But I did it anyway. I couldn't just sort paper, then go home at night and brood.

It was Wednesday morning. I finished performing my *Shaolin* practice, then showered. Bik was nowhere to be seen. My wild dog had not come home last night. I poured some water into one bowl and put some meat scraps in another. I would take the bowls outside and leave them by the side of the building when I left for work. I'd done this before so I expected Bik to find them if she returned.

Now what? I thought. I wasn't due at my desk for another two hours.

As I considered what to do until I left for work, I heard the cry of the produce vendor from the street below. I looked in the icebox and saw I had no fruit except one moderately old lychee. I quickly made out my list, put it and some cash into a basket, and used a rope to lower the basket to the street. This was an age-old practice in our neighborhood, one I had watched my mother perform hundreds of times from our flat two streets away.

I waited a few minutes until the vendor filled my order and had tugged twice on the rope. Then I raised the basket and retrieved the fruit and my change.

One hour later, I sat in my living room reading that morning's edition of the *North China Daily News*. I saw a story on page three of the paper that immediately caught my attention. It told of the murders of three more flower-seller girls and one client over the past four nights.

Although I already knew that these crimes had occurred from the gossip at the station house, I had tried to ignore the news since I was prohibited from looking into them. The investigation had been shut down and, besides, I was marooned on desk duty. Now, however, seeing the details of the crimes, as reported in one place, my involuntarily suppressed concern for Alinka's safety again resurrected itself.

I decided I would have to put my promise to the chief inspector not to investigate the cases on hold, risk my job — if that is what it would take — and secretly investigate and solve the murders, all before Alinka became a target again.

CHAPTER 56

LATE THE NEXT AFTERNOON, JUST before the sun set, Alinka and I met at the Willow Pattern Tea House to share a pot of tea before she left for work. I had something important I wanted to discuss with her, and thought the occasion required a special setting such as this tea house.

The Willow Pattern Tea House had been constructed during the Ming Dynasty. It sat on pilings in the middle of the Whangpoo, and could be reached from the Public Garden only by walking across the Bridge of Nine Turnings, a meandering wooden bridge, with abrupt right turns, designed to frustrate evil spirits who always preferred to travel in a straight line.

We settled into a private room and sat on pillows on the floor facing one another. We were separated by a low, legless table on which sat a tea caddy filled with dried yellow tea, a tea scoop, an urn of boiled, pure spring water, two bowls we would hold with two hands as we sipped our tea, and a lighted candle.

We engaged in small talk as Alinka skillfully prepared and then poured our tea. When she had placed the urn back on the table, I decided to jump right into my reason for inviting her to the tea house.

"Alinka," I said, "I would be honored if you will marry me."

She didn't respond, although I saw a brief flicker of one eyebrow as it briefly arched.

She looked at me as if she wasn't sure she'd heard me correctly.

"Izvinite? — Excuse me? Did I hear you right?*"* She smiled warily and squinted. "You're kidding, Sun-jin, right?" She shook her head once.

When I said nothing to answer her question, she said, "Are you *psyk — psycho?* You know my history, yet you ask me to marry you?"

I found it interesting that she had lapsed back into using some Russian phrases to express her surprise at my request.

I smiled and nodded. "I know your history and I also know you. So, yes, I am asking you to be my wife."

She took a slow, deep breath, held it briefly, then reached across the table and placed her hand on mine.

"You love me very much, don't you?" she said.

I nodded again. I felt her hand briefly squeeze mine.

"Are you offering to marry me so we can be together more often, so you can better protect me?"

"That would be a consequence of our union, but not the reason," I said. "The reason is because I love you, and I want us to spend our lives together."

Alinka looked off in the distance, thinking, obviously, about my request. I assumed she'd never expected this from me.

Alinka considered what life might be like if she married Sun-jin, how her life might change for the better or for the worse. She knew that if she married him, her life could alter in some significant ways she'd never thought about and probably couldn't imagine right now.

She thought about the fact that she would be displayed on his arm when they attended police social functions, as Sun-jin did now, by himself, without her to escort him. She knew she would be expected to dress like an inspector detective's wife, not as a madam, something she could live with.

She knew that in public, as was the Chinese and White Russian custom, she would be expected not to speak unless she was invited to do so, and, then, when she did speak, no one would care what she said. She did not know if she could ever get used to that or if she would want to become used to it. That was not the way things were for her at her sporting house. Everyone there — flower-seller girls, employees, and clients — cared about what she said and thought, or at least they acted as if they did.

She considered all this and mentally shrugged. *Sun-jin, if he wants me to be his wife, will have to forget custom and accept that I will not be a traditional Chinese or a Little Russia wife. The question is: Can he accept that?*

I stared at Alinka, waiting for her answer.

"Alinka—" I said, a tone of wariness evident in my voice. *Perhaps I had misjudged her affection for me.* I picked up my bowl to sip my tea.

"Sun-jin," she said, "if I become your wife, I will not give up my sporting house or my role in it. I will not become like one of those traditional Chinese women or White Russian wives who is confined to her house and family compound, meeting with other similar wives in the obligatory rounds of boring, afternoon visits."

"I wouldn't have it that way," I said.

I felt great relief. She hadn't said no. Not yet. I could live with her conditions, whatever they might be.

"I'll speak my mind in public, no matter who is present," she said, "or whatever the topic. I won't be hushed because I am a policeman's wife."

"I wouldn't expect anything less from you. That's part of your charm."

She looked hard at me — she almost seemed to be looking through me — for what seemed to be a very long minute. It was as if she was weighing my sincerity and the likelihood I would be sorry once we'd married.

She leaned across the table and squeezed my hand. "Then, yes, Sun-jin, if you really mean all that, I will be honored to be your wife."

CHAPTER 57

O F THE FIVE KILLS REQUIRED to complete his assignment, he'd saved the one he most savored for last.

Now he would kill the woman he had attacked at the Happy Times Apartments, the woman whose *Amah* had interrupted them before he could finish her off.

For this kill, he would use his double-wire garrote, the same weapon he had tried to use, but failed with, the last time he attacked her. Now he would especially enjoy himself as the woman would frantically pull at one of the wires, automatically tightening the other, assisting him in bringing about her death. Sin smiled as he pictured the scene.

He considered how he would go about fulfilling this assignment. He realized he'd made a mistake the last time by attacking the woman in her home — in her comfort zone — rather than confronting her at her place of business where she would be distracted and her guard down.

The problem, however, would be to find some way to be alone with her so he could strike the woman. It was not as if he could take the madam of the sporting house to an entertaining room to pillow with him so they would be alone. She was not one of the sporting house's working flower-seller girls.

Sin decided he would make himself a familiar sight at the House of Brilliant Jade by posing as a customer for two nights in a row, before he struck at the woman on the third night.

This he did on those very same nights he'd completed kills three and four, leaving those crime scenes and, being ramped-up with emotion and energy, coming to the House of Brilliant Jade.

There, at Alinka's sporting house, he drank with the women in the parlor, then selected one on each night to pillow with.

He became a familiar face in the parlor those first two nights and, therefore, practically invisible over his three nights there.

CHAPTER 58

ALINKA APPROACHED THE PLANNING OF our wedding with the energy and enthusiasm of a young bride.

I would not have been surprised if, given her heritage, she'd wanted a Russian Orthodox wedding at the Church of the Holy Epiphany, the only Eastern Orthodox church in Little Russia. But that was not to be.

Much to my surprise, since neither of us was wedded to tradition, and since we both prided ourselves on being modern people, knowledgeable about and interested in 1930s' changing trends, Alinka insisted we have an orthodox Chinese wedding. When I asked her why, she merely smiled, shrugged, and said, "It is what I would like, *Spasibo — Thank you.*"

All right. If Alinka wanted a Chinese wedding, with all its contradictions, raucous noise, important elements of face, and its hired participants, I was happy to accede to her wish.

Before she announced this to me, however, I had said to her one morning, "Should we place a notice of our proposed wedding in the White Russian newspapers *Shanghai Zaria* (Shanghai Dawn) and *Slovo* (The Word) to announce our plans to the White Russian community?"

Alinka shook her head. "*Nyet.*"

"Really?" I said.

"Is there some problem, Sun-jin?"

We were sitting in bed in Alinka's flat.

"No, no problem, not at all. I'm surprised, that's all. I didn't say I don't want a traditional wedding festival, Chinese or Eastern Orthodox. I'm not against it. Just surprised."

"Perhaps, Sun-jin, the only surprise should be that you don't know me as well as you think you do."

"Perhaps so, but no matter. If that's what you want, that is what we will have." I paused, then added, "We will, I suppose, learn many new things about one another as we undertake our new relationship."

Alinka smiled, leaned over, and kissed my cheek.

"What do you have in mind for the wedding process," I said, "since we cannot do it all and there are many variations in the tradition?"

"Well, to start, I know what we will not have. We will not have a group of young, howling children jumping and bouncing on our wedding bed to bring us luck in conceiving a child on our wedding night."

I nodded. "I agree. We are too old for such frivolity."

"I'm thinking of making it clear when I invite people that children will not be welcome at our wedding."

I wasn't thrilled about this because I didn't know how Eldest Brother and his wife would react if we banned their children from attending. I decided to put off dealing with this until another day.

"Our wedding will occupy the traditional three days," Alinka said. "During the first two days, we, and those of our guests who are part of the chanting procession, will exchange gifts after our procession has completed its walk through the Settlement.

"I want to have the customary lucky eight men in red costumes, who will bear yokes across their shoulders with hanging baskets on their ends," she said. "I plan to fill the baskets with the usual — some with raw fabrics, some with blankets, some with geese or chickens, some with bowls of lucky gold fish, and others with shrubs and flowers."

I nodded and prudently kept quiet. I thought about the cost of all this, and shuddered. I did not want to be one of those Shanghai bridegrooms who spent ten years after his wedding still paying for its cost. I would put off discussing this for a few days. Now was not the time. This day was for Alinka to revel in her wedding plans.

Alinka leaned over and kissed my cheek.

"Of course our friends," she said, "and such relatives as you invite since I have none, will spend all three days feasting on luxurious foods and watching hired entertainers perform music, juggling, acrobatics, pantomime, puppet shows, dancing, and the like."

She smiled as she seemed to be visualizing the three days.

All at my expense on an inspector-detective's salary and squeeze, I thought.

"Then," she said, "on the third day, as custom requires, I will be brought to the wedding hall in a red, heavily-curtained sedan chair. I will be dressed in a traditional, richly embroidered satin or silk dress. I don't know which yet."

I tried to imagine how beautiful Alinka would be, but could not. I had always avoided attending such events.

"You will be strikingly beautiful," I said.

She smiled. "I will, of course, have to skillfully play the role of a young, blushing bride since, at age twenty-three, I will be neither young nor blushing."

"You will be my young and blushing bride," I said. "I will always see you that way."

Alinka rolled her eyes.

Well, I thought, *that's better than her giving me White Eyes.*

"I will follow tradition and keep my eyes downcast throughout the third day, especially during the marriage ritual. And I will keep my hands folded in the sleeves of my marriage coat."

I was surprised Alinka knew so much about the Chinese wedding tradition. More than I did. Perhaps she learned this when she trained to be a courtesan. I decided to raise this point another day, if at all.

"You will be remarkable," I said.

"After the ceremony, I will remain quiet and demure as my bridesmaid leads me from table-to-table to greet our guests. I will allow my bridesmaid to engage in all the conversation while I stare at my feet and occasionally smile knowingly. As tradition demands, I will say nothing, even if spoken to."

I knew that this latter state of affairs wouldn't continue after the wedding had been completed. I was forewarned.

I reconsidered all the matters I had just decided to put off discussing until another day. There were too many of them accumulating. I decided it was time to assert myself into Alinka's planning, but carefully, and raise a few other points.

"You know, of course, Alinka, my darling, that Generalissimo Chiang Kai-shek and Madam Chiang have instituted wedding reforms as part of their New Life Movement."

"That is of no matter to us," Alinka said. "I am planning for our wedding, not theirs."

"We will be opposing current practices if we avoid the wedding reforms," I said. "Do you really want to do that?"

Alinka stared at me, but said nothing. I could see from the expression on her face that I had waded into dangerous waters.

"What are you saying, Sun-jin?"

"I'm saying that in the spirit of Generalissimo Chiang's reform movement, I was thinking we should have a simpler wedding, a group wedding such as the New Life Movement requires, to be held over two days rather than three. This would be the type of wedding the Kuomintang would help pay for as part of its reform efforts."

Alinka frowned and tapped her foot. "Other than occurring over two days, rather than three, and the government paying for part of the wedding, what else would change?"

"Madam Chiang has suggested that brides should wear simple, white dresses, as Occidentals do in the West, rather than expensive red silk or satin dresses."

"White? Are you crazy? This is my wedding I will be attending, not my funeral. Would you have us in mourning clothes the day our lives are joined and we are about to launch ourselves onto a new path together?"

She paused and frowned. "*Nyet*. White is bad *joss*. I won't have it at my wedding."

I continued, somewhat cautiously now, with my description of a New Life Movement reformed wedding.

"We would be married in a group wedding with fifty or so other couples to save time and costs. And, as I said, the government would pay for part of the wedding ceremony."

Alinka was shaking her head as if she could not believe she was hearing my words. But I wasn't finished yet.

"Generalissimo Chiang has also suggested we do away with buying the expensive, customary ancestral tablets used at traditional weddings, and, instead, have one large portrait of

Sun Yat-sen displayed at the group wedding site. We then all would bow twice before the portrait to show our respect for the state, rather than bow three times before the tablets."

I watched Alinka's face darken.

That was when I struck.

I laughed and held out my hand palm up. She refused to take it.

"Well," I said, as I smiled as brightly as I could, "now that I have performed my civic duty as a SMP Special Branch officer of the city, and have raised the possibility of having a New Life Movement reformed-style wedding, we can ignore my statements concerning reform and get on with planning our traditional wedding, however you wish."

I watched Alinka's face lighten and relax as she started to smile again.

"So, Alinka," I said, "you were telling me about your red wedding dress before I performed my official duty. Will it be silk or satin?"

CHAPTER 59

T U WAITED UNTIL HUANG HAD lit his cigarette for him, then returned to his cushion on the floor to sit opposite Tu's chair.

"Your report, Huang."

"You were correct, Master Tu, as always. The policeman has continued his investigation, but in the evenings, on his own time, even though the Council ordered him to cease."

"Have you tied him to any triad? Do you know who is behind his actions?"

"No, Master Tu. He appears to be acting on his own, without the approval of the SMP or anyone else."

Tu looked across the room, staring at his lucky crickets. He turned back to Huang. His face was dark.

"Someone is driving his investigation. He would not risk his job and career merely to defy his orders. I expect you to find out who is behind the policeman's motivation in this matter."

Huang nodded, then stared at the floor in front of Tu's chair.

"Stay close to the policeman. I expect your answer soon."

CHAPTER 60

S IN CONSIDERED THE MADAM OF the House of Brilliant Jade to be unfinished business. Shortly after the time he'd failed to kill her in her home because her *Amah* interrupted them, he'd asked the master for permission to return to the Happy Times Apartments to try again. For some reason not explained to him, the master refused his request.

Now, with this assignment, the master had given him permission to include that woman among the five people he would kill as part of his assignment at Number Three sporting houses. Sin looked forward to performing this kill. He did not like unfinished business.

Sin, as he had done the previous two nights when he passed himself off as a new customer of the House of Brilliant Jade, dressed as if he was a wealthy comprador. He wore a dark, western-style business suit, a dress shirt, a black cravat, and western-style black shoes. This was his third night at the sporting house.

He entered the front parlor, led there by an elderly greeting-coolie woman. Once in the parlor, he ignored the women and the other men scattered about there, and ordered a drink. He took his seat, alone, and looked over the flower-seller girls as he sipped his beverage.

In accordance with custom, none of the women approached him. They would wait until he signaled one of them to come over and sit by him. When that occurred, he would buy her a drink and he might then also negotiate a price for them to pillow together.

On this third night, Sin sat in the parlor and drank two short glasses of *shaojiu*, without ice. He chain-smoked modern *Yongtai* cigarettes he'd brought with him.

On the two prior occasions when he visited this sporting house, he'd also spent time in the parlor so the women would become familiar and comfortable with him. On those occasions, he ended his nights by selecting a girl, and pillowing with her. He was a generous tipper, a fact now known to all the women.

Tonight, however, he ignored all furtive glances from the flower-seller girls, glances that were intended to catch his eye and have him drink with them.

After he'd consumed his second drink, Sin snuffed out his cigarette in a crystal ashtray provided for the purpose, and said to the nearest flower-seller girl, "Tell the madam of the house I must see her at once."

Alinka appeared in the parlor a few minutes later. She looked around, spotted Sin, and walked over to him. She smiled.

"You asked to see me, sir? How may I be of service?"

Sin stood up from his chair and looked down at Alinka. "I wish to state a complaint."

"*Nichevo? — Really?*" Alinka said. She frowned.

"*Ya nichevo ne znayu — I do not know anything about a problem,*" she thought.

"I am sorry, Uncle, if we have somehow offended you," she said, speaking softly. "Please state your complaint to me so I might remedy it for you."

"It concerns one of your flower-seller girls. I prefer not to speak where we might be overheard," Sin said.

Alinka smiled and nodded. "I understand, but if one of my flower-seller girls has offended you, it will not matter if she overhears us. She will learn of your complaint from me after you leave, and she will no longer be employed here after this night."

"I appreciate that this is as it would be," Sin said, "yet I am not comfortable expressing my unhappiness among strangers. *Qing — Please.* We must have privacy."

Alinka suppressed her annoyance at this new customer who refused to defer to her obvious wishes in her own establishment.

"Very well, Uncle. *Da.* By all means, then," she said, as she smiled, "please follow me to another room where we will be alone."

Alinka, having checked the man's pending, bonded chits for the two other evenings he'd visited her sporting house before she'd entered the parlor to see him, thought, *This is a strange man. He has already spent more on food and drink tonight than he would have to pay for a half-hour with one of my girls.*

CHAPTER 61

ALINKA LED SIN TO A private room on the first floor, away from the front parlor they'd just left, where they would have complete privacy. They would not be overheard or interrupted in this room.

She followed Sin into the room and closed the heavy oak door behind them.

"Please tell me, Uncle," she said, as she faced Sin from one meter away, "how have we offended you."

Sin's left hand shot out toward Alinka. He grabbed her by her throat and tightened his grip. With his right hand, he pulled the garrote from his right pocket and flipped it open, exposing its dual-wire loop.

"Now you will no longer elude me," he said, as he tried to cast the garrote wire over Alinka's bobbing head.

Alinka smelled a familiar odor leaching from the man as he pulled her in close to him. She bit his hand and wrenched herself free from his grip on her throat, then took two steps away from him.

She instinctively assumed the defensive *Kobudo* pose she'd practiced most of her young adult life. Then she prepared to move into the offensive Form. She wished she carried a knife with her, as Sun-jin, from time to time had implored her to do, since *Kobudo* was the martial art that exploited close-in knife fighting.

Sin smiled as he watched Alinka's efforts to set herself to defend herself, and then to attack him. He nodded at her, as if approving her ineffectual effort. He crooked his index finger, figuratively pulling her into him with its *come to me* motion.

Alinka sank her weight into her right leg and prepared to deliver the traditional *Kobudo* kick as soon as Sin moved within range.

He took a step toward her.

Alinka kicked, aiming for Sin's left knee.

Sin brushed the kick away with his left hand. He smiled again.

Alinka was stunned. The man had deflected her aggressive move as casually as he might have swatted away a horsefly that was bothering him.

"Now it is my turn," the man said.

Alinka watched in silence as Sin assumed the posture of the *Wing Chun* Form, a close-in martial art Form that was far more complicated and deadly than *Kobudo*. She knew she had no defense against this Form. She would be helpless to defend herself.

Sin swiftly stepped close in and slammed his right palm into Alinka's nose, crushing the bone and calling forth great gushes of blood.

Alinka stepped back, then fell to the floor, pressing both her hands against her nose. She was blinded by the pain of the break.

Sin moved in closer. He reached down and grabbed Alinka's right arm. He lifted her to her feet.

He moved his hand to Alinka's shoulder, and squeezed so hard that Alinka cried out in pain.

With his free hand, Sin looped the garrote's wires over Alinka's head and slid them down to her neck. With a flick of his wrist, he tightened the wires, than gripped the weapon using both hands. He slowly twisted the handles, further tightening the wires.

Alinka frantically gripped a wire and tried to pull it away from her neck. She squeezed two fingers between her throat and one of the wires. Her efforts were futile. She caused the other wire to tighten.

Sin twisted the handles, tightening the wires. One wire severed Alinka's two fingers at their first knuckle, the fingers that were lodged between her throat and the wire. The other wire cut deeply into her throat.

Sin held the wires tightly, allowing Alinka's slowly slumping body-weight do the work he otherwise would have done by twisting the garrote's handles.

After one minute passed, Sin loosened the garrote, slipped the loop off Alinka's throat and over her head. He watched her melt to the floor.

Alinka didn't move. She did not seem to be breathing.

Sin waited one more minute, then stepped up to Alinka. He pulled back his leg, raised his foot, and kicked Alinka in her ribs as hard as he could. He smiled as he heard bones crack. The woman did not move or cry out.

She was dead.

Sin pocketed the garrote and smiled at the collapsed shape at his feet. He used his palms to smooth back his hair, then adjusted his necktie. He left the House of Brilliant Jade through its back entrance, unnoticed by anyone there.

CHAPTER 62

I was devastated by Alinka's death.

For three days after her murder, while I waited for her body to be released from the official inquest so I could hold her funeral, I was incapable of doing anything other than drinking too much gin, pacing the floor of my flat instead of sleeping, and internally reviewing over and over again the many ways I had failed to protect her.

Eldest Brother stepped in and took charge. He insisted that Bik and I move in with him and his family, and that we stay at their home until after the funeral, if not longer. I agreed, but reluctantly.

Sun-yu sat up with me at night, saying little, but comforting me by his presence. He occasionally told me that Alinka's death was not my fault, that nothing I might have done would have prevented it from occurring, that it was just bad *joss*.

One night, as we waited for Alinka's body to be released to me, Sun-yu said, "Would your woman want a traditional Chinese funeral or a Russian funeral?"

I had no idea, of course, but thought I might know the answer.

"Because Alinka surprised me by wanting a traditional Chinese wedding," I said, "and had never, to my knowledge, shown any interest in the Eastern Orthodox church, I suppose she also would want a traditional Chinese funeral." I shrugged, not fully convinced by my answer.

Eldest Brother nodded.

Sun-yu made all the funeral arrangements, using his own funds, including buying a burial plot in Chapei for Alinka. He also arranged for the customary pomp and ceremony that would precede the funeral in order to provide Alinka with appropriate face.

I took it upon myself to contact a few people who had been in Alinka's life before I knew her. I invited them to her funeral. As far as I knew, her parents were dead, so I made no effort to locate them. But I had heard her mention two individuals I'd never met, so I took the time to locate them and to tell them that Alinka (or, as they knew her, Natalia) had been murdered.

One person was a woman named Maggie File. She had taken in Alinka when Alinka was a child, and had trained her to be a courtesan. The other person was a Frenchman who worked at the *Wing On* department store. He was the makeup artist who taught Alinka how to hide the scar on her face. Alinka had spoken well of both people, so I thought they might honor her memory by attending her funeral rites. Neither person responded to my invitation. Neither attended Alinka's funeral.

On the third day after her death, Alinka's body was released by the police. The funeral procession could now begin.

The morning after Alinka's body was released, we started the two kilometer walk to the cemetery from the public mortuary where she had been kept overnight at Eldest Brother's request.

Sun-yu and I walked behind the coffin, which was carried

by eight coolies hired by Eldest Brother for this purpose. As we walked, Sun-yu and I, as was customary, were shielded from public view on each side by two tall, white cloths that were stretched over wood frames. This contraption was carried by four hired coolies.

We were followed immediately behind by twelve other hired coolies who carried, high above their heads, an elaborately decorated, ten or eleven meters-long, wood and cloth dragon, adorned with gold brocade. These twelve men, in turn, were followed by two dozen other hired coolies who were the official mourners, all dressed in white.

Next, behind the official mourners, came the professional weepers, men and women who were paid to cry and to wail loudly in order to provide maximum noise. This, too, would provide Alinka with face.

Behind the hired weepers and mourners, bringing up the rear, came several cacophonous bands, each made up of ten to twenty musicians. As required by tradition, the bands each made as much noise as possible as we walked, the sound of each band being designed deliberately to conflict with the output of the others in order to drive away evil spirits who, like me, hated their music.

We slowly walked through the narrow streets of the Settlement until we reached the Old City and the outer gate of the cemetery in Chapei. This was where I would bury Alinka.

When we arrived there, the bands and all the hired coolies left the area. Their roles in this ritual were over.

Alinka's coffin was placed next to the excavation that Sun-yu had arranged for.

I stood next to the coffin, with my right palm resting on its top as if I was assuring Alinka that everything would be all right. I was dressed in my best white suit, although it was not a new suit and, since I had purchased it nine or ten years before, did not quite fit me now.

Alinka's burial took place in accordance with Chinese custom. She was removed from her coffin and buried directly in the ground, wrapped in a silk blanket. Then, when this had been completed and the excavation filled in, her coffin was placed above the now filled-in plot, on top of Alinka's grave, to sit there until it would be removed by a relative sometime later.

Since Alinka had no relatives in Shanghai, I would play that role for her. After several weeks, I would arrange to have her empty coffin taken away and given to a charity to be used by some family in need of a free casket.

CHAPTER 63

RETURNED TO WORK TWO DAYS after Alinka's funeral. All I had been able to do at home was pace and wonder why I had failed her.

I didn't see any reason not to go back to my desk to finish out my suspension since I found it difficult to sit home alone, except for the company of Bik. She seemed to sense my deep sorrow, and had stayed close by my side these past two days, even refusing to go outside to do her business unless I accompanied her, as if she didn't trust me to be alone with my thoughts.

As soon as I arrived at the station house and settled in at my desk, I saw a note that had been left there by Chief Inspector Chapman. I read the note, then went to his office to talk to him.

"Good Lord, Sun-jin," he said, as soon as he noticed me hovering in his doorway. "What are you doing here? I left you a note on your desk, but didn't expect you to read it for another week or two when you returned.

"Come in, come in, Dear Boy. Sit." He waved me over to the chair in front of his desk.

We made small talk. He commiserated with me concerning

Alinka's death, and again said he was surprised to see me back at work so soon.

"I want to reopen the flower-seller girls' investigation," I said, "beginning with Alinka's murder."

"I'm not surprised," he said. "but you know what we're up against with the order from the Council. Sorry, but I cannot allow it."

I shifted in my seat. "Sir, I'm either going to do it officially with your blessing or I am going to do it unofficially. But, either way, I'm going to do it."

"You'll be fired if you go off on your own, Sun-jin," he said. "I'd rather you not put me in a position where I have to do that."

"That would be regrettable sir," I said, "but I'd live with it if it came to that. I intend to find the killer, one way or the other."

The chief inspector stared at me, but said nothing.

"It would be better for me to still have a job when this is over, and better, too, for the SMP to have me, as an experienced inspector detective, still working for it, but I can live with the outcome, either way. I know what I have to do."

The chief inspector nodded, but still said nothing.

"However it must be, sir, I am going to pursue this."

The chief inspector stood up and walked around from behind his desk to his office door. He closed the door, then returned to his seat, slowing briefly as he passed by me to pat my shoulder twice.

"All right, Sun-jin, I understand, but you will have to follow some rules."

I didn't say anything. I needed to know what he had in mind.

He fell silent and stared briefly at his desktop.

I waited.

"I insist you be discreet," he said. "Very discreet. If it leaks out what you're up to, we're both finished here. We'll both be sacked."

"Yes, sir. I know that."

"You will investigate entirely on your own, outside the SMP's procedures. No reports, and no meetings that involve anyone who might figure out what you're up to. Talk only to me, if you need a sounding board or need something from the files.

"You will officially be on leave, in mourning," he said, "so no one will expect you to appear at your desk. Therefore, don't."

I nodded.

"Keep me informed at all times. I don't want any surprises. None."

"Yes, sir," I said, my spirits lifting.

"Before you start, figure out some plausible cover for yourself in case someone learns you're back to investigating the murders, then stick to it.

"Talk to me often. Do not — and I mean, *do not* — keep me in the dark. Again, I do not want any surprises from anywhere, especially from the Council. When you report to me, we will meet at the Willow Pattern Tea House to talk. Not here."

"Yes, sir. I understand."

"Before you leave, take everything you might need, files, maps, whatever. Do not come back here for anything while you're carrying on the investigation."

With that, the chief inspector stood. He leaned across his desk and thrust out his hand to shake mine.

"Good luck, Inspector Detective. Find whoever killed your woman, and bring him to justice for all his victims."

CHAPTER 64

RESUMED MY INVESTIGATION. I FELT relieved, under the circumstances, that I no longer had to hide my intentions, actions or thoughts from my boss. I only had to keep him informed, be circumspect, and not be found out by others.

Even better, for the first time since I was assigned the first murder at the House of Multiple Joys, I was not answerable to anyone for my progress or lack of it. Only to myself and to Alinka's memory.

I decided to revisit each of the sporting houses where the killings had occurred. Hopefully, with the passage of time and the dissipation of the original shock caused by the crimes, someone might now recall some fact they hadn't told me before.

I decided, however, I would not revisit the House of the Ascending Sun. I didn't expect any of the Dwarf Bandits there to cooperate with me, and I did not want Harue to find out I had opened the investigation again. He might report it to the JCP or, even worse, to the SMP.

I started with the Temple of Supreme Happiness.

The sporting house's madam seemed indifferent to my return visit. It was as if the murder had happened so long ago as to now be but a distant, not very important, memory, or as if such occurrences were routine. She merely shrugged when I asked her to repeat her memory of the murder and the night it occurred.

She reluctantly complied as if I were imposing a great burden on her, and that by doing so, I was taking her away from her more important, current duties.

She repeated, albeit with less specificity than before, what she told me during the earliest days of the investigation. She added nothing new.

I then went upstairs to the entertaining room of the flower-seller girl who had found the victim to re-interview her. In the end, there was nothing new there, either.

I returned downstairs to ask the madam one other question that had occurred to me.

"Auntie," I said, "has anything unusual occurred since the time of the crime? Even anything that seemed unrelated, but struck you as out of the ordinary at the time?"

She shook her head, more, it seemed to me, as a reflection of her disinterest in being questioned, than as a response to my question.

I stood my ground, didn't turn to leave.

"Anything at all, Auntie?" I repeated.

She shook her head again. This time she also gave me White Eyes. She'd lost patience with me. I was getting nowhere with her.

I started to put away my notebook when she said, "Nephew, there was one thing, both before and again soon after the murder, but it probably was unrelated." She shrugged.

"What was that?" I asked without much enthusiasm.

"A young man, probably from a triad by his dress and

manner of disrespect, came to see me a week or more before the murder, then again after the murder. Both times he said he wanted to buy my sporting house."

Now that was something new.

"Buy your business or buy the land and house itself?" I said.

"The land and the mansion," she said. "I told him both times it was not for sale and, the second time, chased him away with my broom."

"Was he a round eye or Chinese?" I said, although from her previous reference to a triad, I thought I knew what her answer would be.

"A Celestial Being."

"Why do you think this might be connected to the murder?" I asked.

"Because when I told him I was not interested in selling, before I chased him away, he said, in a voice so soft I am not sure I was meant to hear him, 'But you will be interested, Auntie, sooner, rather than later.' I took that to be a threat."

I left the Temple of Supreme Happiness feeling I had come across an important piece of information, although I had no idea yet what it meant or what I should do with it.

From the Temple of Supreme Happiness, I went to the other sporting houses that had been crime scenes.

The current madam of the House of Fragrant Pleasures described a similar encounter at her sporting house two weeks before and again one week after the murder of the former madam there.

I next went to the House of Brilliant Jade.

Although I obviously could not ask Alinka if she'd had a

similar encounter, I could ask her executrix who was winding-down the business and who would ultimately close the sporting house, acting under Alinka's Last Will and Testament.

The woman indicated that, yes, Alinka had been approached twice to sell her property, before and after the two murders at the mansion. She had complained to this woman about it, and had refused to agree to sell.

I then checked with the madams of the four sporting houses where the most recent murders had occurred over one week, and found out that they, too, had been approached by a young Chinese man who offered to buy their properties. Again, before and after the murders at their houses.

That left only Gracie Gale at the House of Multiple Joys to be checked.

Gracie and I settled into a backroom parlor on the ground floor. She served us each a glass of wine, and offered me a fine cigar.

I saw no reason not to be direct with her. Gracie was honorable; I trusted her; and, I had a specific goal in mind — to firm up the pattern I'd seen emerging at the other sporting houses where murders had occurred.

I told her about my current, unofficial, secret status as an investigator. Then I asked her the key question.

"Did anyone approach you about buying your business or this building and land after the two murders here?" I said.

"My business? No," she said, "but a young man, who would not disclose who he represented, asked me to sell the land and building one week or so before the murder. He also asked me again one week after the murder of my girl. I said no both times. Why do you want to know?"

CHAPTER 65

I WASN'T SURE WHAT THIS NEW information might mean to my investigation, what impact it might have if it did fit in, or what I should do with it if it turned out to be relevant. I had a nagging fear that this information might have nothing at all to do with the crimes, that it might just reflect someone taking advantage of the adverse situations at the sporting houses, resulting from the murders, to acquire valuable real estate at reduced prices. I worried about reading too much into this information and leading myself off in the wrong direction.

In spite of my misgivings, because I clearly hadn't gotten far with my traditional-style investigation, I decided to pursue the path suggested by this new information and see where it might lead me. I would do this by trying to learn if there had been similar offers made at other sporting houses where killings had not occurred.

If any of these other sporting houses had received offers to buy their properties, but no murders had occurred there, that likely would eliminate this new information as a legitimate line of inquiry for me.

———◈———

I spent the afternoon visiting and questioning the madams of eighteen sporting houses that were in the vicinity of the houses where killings had occurred. None of these houses had had a murder occur there.

All eighteen madams were reluctant to speak with me until I threatened to use my authority as an inspector detective to arrest them for hindering my investigation. I also said I would shut-down their sporting houses if they did not cooperate.

Five of the eighteen sporting houses had not received offers to buy their real estate. The other thirteen had received offers. Of these thirteen, nine houses had accepted the offers and agreed to sell their properties. Four still were considering the offers. None of the thirteen had turned down the offers.

The madams of the thirteen houses that had received offers were warned not to mention the offers to anyone. They claimed that they were told that if they discussed the offers, even if they just mentioned the existence of the offers, the offers would be reduced by fifty percent.

When I finished my interview with the last madam, I considered why someone would insist on keeping the offers secret. I concluded that doing so was a means to control the prices the person who made the offers would have to pay for each subsequent sporting house he approached to buy. And, having concluded that, I also realized that this would be relevant only if that person wanted to buy many parcels of land in the same general location so he could assemble them into one large parcel of real estate.

Assuming I was correct, I decided to widen my inquiry to include other sporting houses that were located near the Bund, but not too close to the eighteen sporting houses I had just finished visiting, or close to the sporting houses where murders had occurred.

That afternoon, I visited eleven other sporting houses. None had received an offer. None had had a murder occur there.

I returned home and took out a large street map of the International Settlement I had purchased at *Wing On* department store to use in my investigation. I pinned it to the kitchen wall.

I marked the word "Yes" in bright red crayon at the location of each of the sporting houses where one or more murders had occurred. Each of these sporting houses had two things in common: each had received an offer to buy its real estate and each had turned down the offer before the murder occurred.

I next placed a large red question mark at the location of the House of the Ascending Sun since I did not know if a similar offer had been made to the madam of that Japanese house. I had no intention of inquiring about this right now since I did not want Harue to learn I was again investigating the killings.

I then marked the words "No Offer" in red on the map at the location of each of the last eleven sporting house where I had made an inquiry, but where no killings had occurred. None of these sporting houses had received an offer to buy their real estate.

Finally, I wrote the word "OK" in red on the map to indicate the thirteen sporting houses that had received offers, but had not had a killing occur on their sites. These houses had either accepted the offers to buy their properties or were still considering the offers. None had rejected the offer. I noted that these sporting houses were randomly intermingled among the sporting houses that had been crime scenes near the Bund, along the Line.

I was pretty sure I understood what was going on. Now, I just had to figure out who was involved.

I decided to visit Big-Eared Tu again to see if he would shed any light on my theory. I assumed he could do so if he wanted to, but I wondered if he would do so.

CHAPTER 66

WHEN I ARRIVED AT TU'S house, he again received me in his Great Room.

"Thank you for allowing me to visit with you again, Master Tu. Especially this time, since I did not make an appointment. I know you are a busy man."

"You are always welcome in my home, Inspector Detective."

We sat across from one another, separated by a low table made of highly-polished boxwood. A kettle of tea and two empty cups sat in its center. The sounds of Tu's lucky crickets and songbirds filled the room.

"To what do I owe the pleasure of your unexpected visit?"

I described the pattern I'd seen among the sporting houses where killings had occurred. I also described the patterns in the two groups of eighteen and eleven other sporting houses I'd visited, pointing out that murders had occurred only at sporting houses where an offer to buy had been made and had been rejected.

"Do you know anything about this, Master Tu?"

"It was my understanding that the Council has ended this investigation you are conducting. Are you again authorized to ask me these questions?"

"I am not, sir, but that was before, Master Tu. Circumstances have changed. I would appreciate your answer to my question."

For some reason, this time when I met with him, I did not feel intimidated by Tu or reluctant to speak up in his presence. I knew I would not receive any answers from him if I continued to play the role of the deferential supplicant. I had to push him hard if I was going to find out from him if he had any information I needed to know.

Tu put his hand in a pocket of his gown and pulled out a small bell which he rang. A servant promptly entered the Great Room, as if he had been poised outside the door ready to come in when he heard Tu's signal. Tu instructed him to pour our tea.

When the servant left and had closed the door, Tu picked up his cup, held it between the palms of his hands, and slurped his tea, emptying the steaming cup. I did not touch my cup, but stared at Tu as he performed his diversionary ritual.

When he finally spoke, Tu said, "I do not know anything specifically about this, but I have heard indirectly that someone important has an interest in seeing that the offers are fulfilled.

"What I also know is that these trivial incidents do not seek to impinge on my business or authority, in general, so they do not concern me. I cannot see any reason, therefore, why you should contact me again about these matters."

That was valuable information — the part about an important person being involved — coming as it did from Tu, whose sources would be reliable.

"Do you know who that person is?" I said.

"I do not. If I did, I likely would not tell you."

That did not surprise me.

"Why do you continue your investigation against the

Council's orders?" Tu said. "Is someone encouraging you to do so?"

It did not surprise me that Tu knew I'd been told to stop my investigation. It did surprise me, however, that he had not determined my reason for not following orders.

"Because I have to atone for my failure to protect my woman from the murderer."

Tu nodded. "I see."

"Will you help me, Master Tu?"

Tu shook his head, then stood up. My visit was over.

As soon as Sun-jin left the Great Room, Pock-Marked Huang stepped through a door that had been partly closed.

"It will be interesting, Master Tu, to observe how the policeman reacts to the information you offered him."

CHAPTER 67

I LEFT TU AND RETURNED HOME to think about what I had learned so far and to plan my next step in the investigation.

The first thing I did at home was feed Bik and refill her water bowl. When she finished eating and drinking, I let her go outside to play at being a wild dog.

After Bik left, I turned back to my investigation.

I created an image in my mind of what I thought the man who made the offers to the madams might look like. I based this on the information I had obtained from the madams who had seen him and from the girls who had talked with him in the parlors, or who had pillowed with him.

The descriptions were as consistent as could be expected given the passage of time and the general unreliability of eye witnesses. They were not consistent at all.

Some witnesses said the man was Chinese; others that he was European. Most said he was about twenty-five to thirty years old, stood approximately 1.9 meters tall, weighed about 61 kg, and had black hair worn in a western style. All agreed he had a clean-shaven face. The consensus was that he was trim, but muscular.

The madams all said that he was well-spoken. It seemed he used Mandarin as his dialect for madams who were Chinese and used English for those madams who were Occidental. This told me he likely was educated. None of the flower-seller girls could remember his voice.

The witness's disagreement whether the man was Oriental or was Caucasian caught my attention.

I thought about the composite description I'd received and now carried in my mind's eye. I could almost picture the man. *He certainly did not resemble the various descriptions of the man who had pillowed with flower-seller girls or who drank liquor at several sporting houses before killing Alinka and some of his other victims. That man seemed to be younger and more athletic than the man who had made offers to the madams. Besides, all the flower-seller girls who had pillowed with him said he was Chinese. Not one disagreed concerning that matter.*

Given these insights, it appeared I was dealing with two men.

Were they both involved in the crimes? I wondered. *Did they have separate roles to play in this matter — one to make the offers to buy, the other to coerce people into selling their properties and to kill them or other people if they would not sell?*

Assuming I was correct that I was looking for two men, I decided to try to locate and interview the man who had offered to buy the sporting houses. He would seem to be the less culpable of the two men, and, therefore, the most likely of the two to be willing to speak with me. I would deal with his accomplice later. If I was successful in finding the man who made the offers, he might lead me to his accomplice.

I placed small display notices in the *North China Daily News*, the *Shanghai Times*, and the *Mercury China Press*, all English-language newspapers read by foreigners and educated Chinese alike.

My notice was simple:

> Want to meet with man who made offers to buy sporting houses in the Settlement and also in the French Concession. Believe we can be mutually helpful to one another. Telephone me at 70141.

I ran the notice in each paper, every day for one week. I did not expect to receive a response, and I was not disappointed. I never heard from the man.

CHAPTER 68

A LITTLE MORE THAN ONE WEEK after I ran the notices in the newspapers to contact the man who had made offers to the madams, I defied the chief inspector's order to me and I returned to my office for the first time since undertaking my clandestine investigation. I needed a change of scenery.

I made it up the back stairs and into my office without running into anyone who knew me. I kept my door closed while there.

I stood before the wall map and noted the markings I had made while at home indicating sporting houses that had received offers to buy their properties. I ignored for now whether or not murders had occurred at any of these houses.

I took my red crayon and drew a thick boundary line along the perimeter of the cluster, dragging the line from one outermost sporting house that had received an offer to buy to the next one, ignoring all those that fell inside this crayon boundary I was drawing. I wanted to create an outer perimeter line that would surround all of the relevant sporting houses. This resulted in a rough oval shape that encompassed approximately two and one-half city blocks.

I considered what could be built on such a large parcel. *A house with much land surrounding it? Yes, it could be built, but who would want such an estate so close to the Bund, in the middle of the*

Settlement's commercial and financial district? No one, I decided. That type project would be more suited to the French Concession.

A large hotel? Perhaps, but no one would want to pay the price for this much land just for a hotel. Real estate developers Sidney J. Powell and Brenan Atkinson had shown that this was not necessary when they built their luxury hotels — the Medhurst Hotel on Bubbling Well Road and the Park Hotel, also on Bubbling Well Road — placing each on much smaller parcels near the Bund. Even Tug Wilson, the notorious master architect and real estate developer, had done the same thing when he built the luxurious Palace Hotel nearby. His parcel amounted to much less than that drawn on my wall map.

I thought about where this was leading me. *A large, horizontal retail emporium, perhaps? But this much land would not be necessary,* I thought as I stared at the wall map I'd brought along from home. *The very tall, successful Wing On department store located on a small parcel on Nanking Road, had proven that much.*

These projects, although differing in their uses, had one thing in common: they all sat on small parcels of land and were built upward, vertically stretching their useable areas as high as possible. None of these — or any projects similar to them — had required the assemblage of many small parcels into one huge parcel, based on the nature of their designs.

I didn't have an answer to my question. I wondered what I had missed. I walked over to the bookshelf and retrieved my copy of the popular Shanghai visitor's guidebook, All About Shanghai/A Standard Guidebook, published in English last year. I took the book, sat down behind my desk, and started turning pages. I hoped I would see something that would strike me as relevant.

I found the answer on pages fifty-three and fifty-four of the guidebook.

CHAPTER 69

CCORDING TO THE GUIDEBOOK, THE only currently
existing structure in Shanghai that required a parcel almost
as broad as the one now indicated by the irregular red oval
I'd created on my wall map was the Hongkew Market, sitting,
as it did, on one square city block of land.

I immediately left my office and went to the building next
door — to the Hall of Records — to examine the building
permit and construction plans on file for the Hongkew Market.

According to the official records, the land under the Hongkew
Market had required that twenty-seven small parcels of land be
assembled into one large parcel. By my calculation, the boundary
schematic for the Hongkew Market, if it were superimposed on
my wall map oval, would occupy only about seventy percent of
the parcel shown by the red boundary line I had drawn.

Someone was assembling parcels for a very large project,
one that would dwarf the Hongkew Market in its overall area.

I believed I now understood the motive behind the sporting
house murders.

A murder had been committed in every house in which
the madam had rejected an offer to buy her property, but
murders had not been committed in the thirteen houses where
the madams either had accepted the offers to buy or still were
considering the offers.

CHAPTER 70

N OW THAT I UNDERSTOOD WHY the murders had been committed — to intimidate the madams into selling their sporting houses and the land under them, and possibly also to punish those madams who had rejected the offers to buy — I next had to figure out who was behind this scheme.

Who, I wondered, *even had the capacity to do this, to build a structure as large as or larger than the Hongkew Market in the middle of the International Settlement?*

I knew the names of the most prominent real estate builders in Shanghai: Sidney J. Powell, Brenan Atkinson, Tug Wilson, Victor Sassoon, and Bright Fraser. As I thought about it, based on their track records and ownership of properties, I decided that only Wilson and Sassoon had the capacity — based on their experience, their current massive ownership of realty, and their reputed general assets — to develop a retail project of this magnitude during the worldwide Depression that had come to Shanghai this past year.

But both Tug Wilson and Victor Sassoon were unlikely candidates to be the power behind the murders. Not only did they not have to acquire property this way, they apparently had done business just fine without resorting to such crimes or to such strong-arm tactics. They both had superb reputations as honest, if not fiercely competitive, businessmen. I thought it a desperate stretch on my part to think they might be involved.

Yet the more I thought about it, the more I thought maybe I was being too generous to them by so readily dismissing them as suspects.

Would either Wilson or Sassoon have done this? Would they even have needed to resort to such tactics to acquire the properties?

I didn't know. I was skeptical, but not as ready as before to dismiss their involvement without more information. What I needed was evidence exonerating them or evidence pulling them in, if that was the case. Not speculation based on their general reputations and success as real estate developers and project operators.

Would they have hired a killer to coerce madams into selling their properties? Maybe I had to reconsider the possibility one of them was involved behind the scenes.

I spent the rest of the day turning these questions over in my mind. I eventually deviated from my earlier position. I decided that, yes, either one of these two men might have undertaken this nefarious, coercive program, and that I could not just dismiss them as possibilities without more information.

I decided that if either Wilson or Sassoon was involved, he would have used someone else to do the dirty work for him, to run the scheme on a day-to-day basis. I couldn't imagine either Wilson or Sassoon dirtying his own hands to undertake this extortive and punitive campaign. He would use cutouts so he could distance himself from the crimes if the scheme ever came to light.

Having come to this conclusion, I next considered the way Wilson or Sassoon might have implemented the program.

How, I wondered, *would Wilson or Sassoon find some third party he could sufficiently trust to perform the killings and to protect him from ever being implicated if the conspiracy was discovered?*

I thought about this and found the answer in the very nature of British/Chinese societal and business relationships that were all around me.

The only person who could be trusted to take this on for either Wilson or Sassoon would have to be someone he already fully trusted based on his prior dealings with that person.

The only person I could imagine who would fit this narrow description, because of the inherent nature of the relationship — personal and business — would be a taipan's comprador.

But Tug Wilson was not a taipan. That meant he did not have a special relationship with a comprador. I doubted he had such a relationship with anyone else who might commit multiple murders for him.

Victor Sassoon, however, was a taipan. He did have a comprador in whom he had already placed his trust, someone who already held the taipan's personal and business lives in his hands. Comprador Chen Bao.

CHAPTER 71

THE TIME HAD COME FOR me to report to Chief Inspector Chapman, to tell him my conclusions and how I had arrived at them. We arranged to meet the next morning at the Willow Pattern Tea House.

"That's preposterous," the chief inspector said. "Don't even think that," he added, "let alone say it out loud."

I watched the chief inspector's face redden and his forehead dampen as beads of sweat formed on this brow. He snorted once and abruptly shook his head.

"Damn you, Sun-jin. I knew I shouldn't have let you go on with your investigation. You're going to get us both fired."

I remained quiet as the chief inspector spewed steam.

"Well, that does it for you," he said. "I prohibit you from continuing your investigation and from sharing your absurd ideas with anyone else. Not with anyone," he said. "Understand?"

He shook his head, frowned again, and added, "And don't even think about questioning the taipan or his comprador. Or, worse, arresting them. It's our jobs now that are at stake.

"I'm sorry about your lady friend," he said, "you know that, but I'm closing down your investigation before you go too far. Come back to work when you're ready, but you'll be back at your desk for now."

CHAPTER 72

T U THOUGHT ABOUT HIS MEETING earlier that morning with Sun-jin. He believed what the policeman had said.

He was driven by his need to make up for his failure to protect his damaged whore, Tu thought.

Tu reconsidered his earlier decision to have Huang watch the policeman. It no longer was necessary. The policeman had his own agenda to fulfill with his investigation. He was not acting on behalf of someone else trying to bring down Tu.

Satisfied he was correct, based on his conversation with the foolish policeman and by the failure of Huang to uncover anything contrary, he thought, *I can leave the policeman to his fruitless investigation. He is not a threat to me.*

CHAPTER 73

I LEFT THE CHIEF INSPECTOR SITTING at the tea house. He didn't want anyone to see us together as he headed back to the station house.

I was frustrated and angry. I didn't know if the chief inspector was covering up for the guilty party, or if he just was concerned with keeping his job, as he'd indicated, or, both. In any event, it was too late to put the brakes on my investigation now that I had a realistic working theory why the murders had been committed. I now believed that given more time to pursue this, I would solve the crimes and avenge Alinka's death.

I decided to risk losing my job. I no longer cared. I would continue to investigate the murders and would deal with any problems that might later arise from that.

───◦─◦─❁─◦─◦───

I headed home. I wanted time to think about what I had learned so far, consider any alternative theories based on the evidence I had turned up, and see if my conclusions still made sense in the cold light of day. I needed to perform this last mental check before I defied the chief inspector's order and started down the path that likely would end my career as an SMP policemen, but might bring justice to Alinka and the other Flowery Kingdom victims.

Although it was mid-day, I poured myself a glass of Cheefoo beer, and settled in at the table in my kitchen. I had brought the wall map home from the tea house. I spread it out across the kitchen table. I looked at all the notes I had entered onto the map and, specifically, at the red boundary line I had drawn that circumscribed one large, assembled parcel.

Bik had been sitting on the front stoop of the apartment building when I arrived home. She followed me in the door and up the steps to our flat. Now, she was curled up and sleeping under the table, her snout and head resting firmly against my right foot. I tried not to move too much so I wouldn't disturb her.

Thirty minutes later, I refolded the map and put it away. I had no doubt my conclusion was correct. The map showed it to be so. Someone was attempting to assemble the small sporting house parcels of land into one large parcel. Why? Clearly to build something large on it, to be located within a short walk to or from the Bund. Something that would be commercial and valuable.

I also believed my research was correct when I concluded that only a horizontal, commercial project as large as, or larger than, the Hongkew Market made sense near the Bund.

And, finally, I also believed that only one person in Shanghai had the experience, the financial, and the business resources to pull off such a large project in the current, depressed economic climate. That person was Taipan Victor Sassoon.

If I was correct, and I had no doubt I was, then my next question was: who would have organized the killings, intimidation, and assembling of the parcels on behalf of the taipan?

That answer, too, was obvious to me. As I'd already

concluded: Victor Sassoon's comprador, the well-known, well-connected, very rich, and former martial arts teacher, Chen Bao.

But, I thought, *if Chen Bao was so well-known, was so well-connected, and so very rich, why would he become involved in such crimes and risk destroying his life and everything he had if he were found out? It made no sense.*

Or did it?

In my years as a policeman, both as a patrolman and later as an investigator, I'd learned not to underestimate the corrosive influence on lives of greed and of the quest for power that some men had. Even when they already possessed these attributes. Some such men often craved even more, having had some taste of power and wealth.

I tried to put myself in Chen Bao's place to see how he might act.

What I concluded — and I had no doubt I was correct — was that Chen Bao had decided that as he caused his taipan to become more powerful and wealthier, that he, too, as his taipan's comprador, would become more powerful and, perhaps, even wealthier. He likely also believed that as a result, he also would have more influence in the Chinese community than he already had. He would thrive in the reflected glory, influence, and power of his taipan.

And that, I decided, was the basis for Chen Bao's participation in the deaths in the Flowery Kingdom.

CHAPTER 74

TWO DAYS AFTER OUR MEETING at the tea house, as a courtesy to Chief Inspector Chapman because he had supported my efforts to uncover the perpetrators of the murders after Alinka died, I decided I had no choice but to go back to him and report what I'd concluded. I also would tell him what I intended to do with this knowledge. I owed him that much.

I understood that by telling him I intended to arrest Chen Bao and Victor Sassoon, I would be putting my job as an inspector detective at risk, that he might immediately fire me, removing my authority to officially follow through with my plan. But I also knew I had to take that risk. I trusted that the chief inspector would see the necessity of enforcing the law against the comprador and taipan, that he would demonstrate the required courage and integrity to authorize me to do so, and would clear me to proceed because, deep down, he was a conscientious policeman.

"You want to do what? Are you out of your mind?" The chief inspector's face had turned bright crimson. He shook his head several times as he scowled at me.

"Please, sir, just allow me to walk you through my investigation and show you how I reached the conclusions I've arrived at." I unfolded the wall map I had carried with me to his office.

With his permission, I spread the map across his desktop. It took me fifteen minutes to take the chief inspector from one end of my investigation to its conclusion. He did not ask any questions while I spoke.

When I finished by stating that only Taipan Victor Sassoon and Chen Bao could be the people behind the murders, the chief inspector said nothing. I could see him considering what I'd said.

He filled his pipe, lit it, and puffed on the burning tobacco, still saying nothing.

After another minute passed, he said, "No, Sun-jin, you do not have my permission to arrest the comprador or the taipan. You don't have enough evidence to justify it, just theory."

I had expected him to say that. I actually agreed with him, but did not say so. I had achieved my objective with the chief inspector. Now I tried to appear as if I was both disappointed and angered by his decision.

Not having enough evidence, I thought, *was better than having no evidence, and better, too, than again being prohibited from pursuing more evidence.* The chief inspector's concluding statement implicitly gave me permission to go out and find more evidence.

I left Chief Inspector Chapman's office feeling once again that I had achieved a small victory in my quest.

CHAPTER 75

DECIDED TO MAKE AN UNANNOUNCED visit to Chen Bao at his home on L'Avenue du Roi in the French Concession.

Before I did this, however, I spent part of the afternoon in the newspaper archives reading everything I could find written about the comprador — his business relationship with his taipan and the *hong* he worked for (E. D. Sassoon & Company), his extended family, his other businesses not involving the *hong*, his investments and assets, and, above all else, his personality and reputation.

Among other things, I discovered that Chen Bao seemed to have a very good relationship with Victor Sassoon, and that he had great wealth, much of it consisting of homes in Shanghai, Amoy, and Hong Kong.

———❖———

The next morning, I showed up unannounced at the front door of Chen Bao's Frenchtown home, intentionally not having made an advance appointment to meet with him.

Chen Bao was gracious. He welcomed me into his home, never mentioning my social, business, and Confucian blunders of having failed to obtain an appointment before showing up.

When we'd settled into his Great Room, Chen Bao looked

at me and said, "Why are you here, Inspector Detective? How may I be of assistance to you?"

"I have some questions concerning the sporting house murders," I said.

He shook his head slowly. "What could I possibly know that I could tell you?"

I told him how he could help me, setting out my theory of the cases.

He seemed amused by my statements, but also dismissive of me, until I said that I believed he was fronting for Victor Sassoon.

Chen's face turned sullen as he took a slow, deep breath. He abruptly stood up and pointed his finger at me.

"You dare come into my home and insult my taipan? You have no idea who it is you are dealing with or what you have to lose by your insults and accusations.

"You will go now, Inspector Detective. Leave my home and do not return again."

The comprador was furious.

After Sun-jin left, Chen Bao dialed a familiar telephone number.

"This is the master," he said, when Sin answered the call.

CHAPTER 76

THE NEXT MORNING, CHEN BAO knocked once on the taipan's office door, then entered when Sassoon said, "Come."

He felt less than secure concerning what he was about to tell his taipan.

After they discussed some ordinary business matters, Chen Bao said, "We have a possible problem, Taipan."

Chen Bao described his recent meeting with Sun-jin.

Victor Sassoon remained sitting behind his desk, listening to his comprador, taking it all in without interrupting.

When it became clear that the comprador was finished speaking, Sassoon said, "This won't be a problem. I will make some telephone calls, and will suggest, among other things, that I am considering foreclosing the mortgage against the Shanghai Club's property unless I receive the Council's full support in shutting down the inspector detective's investigation once and for all. The Council will bury the whole matter rather than lose the Shanghai Club to me."

Chen Bao rubbed his palms together. "That should be satisfactory, Taipan."

"In the unlikely event there still remains some problem,"

Sassoon said, "and if for some reason you should be taken into custody, I expect you to fully protect me."

"Of course, Taipan."

"Your reward for doing so will well satisfy you," Sassoon said. "I can assure you of that."

"I have no doubt," Chen Bao said. He bowed his head slightly.

CHAPTER 77

THE MASTER WAS VERY CLEAR when he gave Sin his new assignment.

"Do not use the bow and arrow. It is too impersonal. Do not use poison. It also is too impersonal. You may use the garrote, he'd said, but I would prefer you do not. It is too quick.

"I want you to use your knife on the policeman in such a way as to cause him to die slowly."

Sin nodded.

"When it is clear to you that he is dying, I want you to tell him that I was the person who ordered his death, identifying me by my birth name when you tell him."

"Yes, Master."

"As he dies, while his mind still is able to comprehend what you are saying, be sure to tell him you were the weapon I sent to remove his defective woman from this life, so that this thought will be the last thing he knows before he dies."

CHAPTER 78

S IN KNOW WHERE IN THE Old City the policeman lived. The master had given him this information. He also knew, because he had eliminated the whore from the policeman's life, that the policeman lived alone.

Sin watched the policeman's home from across the road, waiting until the sun had set. He continued to watch until the light went out in the policeman's second-floor window.

He waited until 3:00 a.m. Then, using his lock-picking tools to gain entrance to the apartment building's front door, Sin pushed aside a mangy dog that tried to enter the front door with him, and quietly walked into the policeman's apartment building.

He placed his ear against Sun-jin's door. There was no sound from within and no light from the interior room stealing out under the door.

He again removed his lock-picking tools from his pocket, then disengaged the door's lock. He quietly entered Sun-jin's flat.

He saw another door, partly closed, across the living room. It likely was the door to the policeman's bedroom.

Sin quietly eased the door further open and peered in. He saw the policeman in bed, sleeping.

He crept in.

As he neared the bed, he unsheathed his knife.

When Sin was within striking distance of the sleeping figure, Sun-jin suddenly rolled over, away from Sin, and leaped out of bed. He held a pistol in his right hand. The bed separated the two men.

Sin dropped to the floor and rolled under the edge of the bed just before Sun-jin fired a shot at him. The bullet lodged in the wall behind where Sin had just been standing.

Sin leaped up onto his feet, facing Sun-jin.

As Sun-jin pulled back the hammer and took aim to shoot again, Sin buried his head in his chest and leaped against the window, crashing his shoulder and the top of his head into the breaking glass and splintering wood frame. He dropped two stories toward the ground, then tucked and rolled as he touched down.

Sun-jin looked out his broken window and watched the intruder hobble away from the building.

He also saw Bik standing in the moonlight looking up at him, her tail wagging.

CHAPTER 79

WAS INFURIATED BY THE ATTEMPT on my life. Clearly it was meant to discourage me from pursuing my investigation or to close me down permanently by killing me. It told me I was getting too close to whoever was behind the crimes for them to remain comfortable. My anger fueled my desire to move ahead with my investigation.

I was not yet ready to confront Sassoon. The taipan had too much influence in Shanghai, in spite of being a detested Hebrew among the other rich and powerful men in the city.

In the morning, I went back to Chen Bao's home. He reluctantly agreed to see me again even though I was defying his order never to return to his house.

"What is it you want now, Mr. Policeman. Haven't we talked your investigation to death?" Chen had skipped the required, preliminary Confucian talk.

"I'm here to arrest you. Put your hands behind your back and turn around toward me." I removed a pair of adjustable handcuffs from my belt where they'd been hanging.

Chen Bao, rather than being upset or angry, as I'd expected

him to be, seemed amused. He did not turn around as I'd ordered him to do.

"You should think before you act, Mr. Policeman. Your job and possibly your freedom are at risk."

"Turn around," I said, holding up the handcuffs.

He complied.

I cuffed him and took him back to the station house.

The chief inspector threw a fit.

His face lost all its color. I could see his mind racing. He seemed panicked.

"Stay here until I return," he said. He slammed the door on his way out.

When the chief inspector returned, he told me he had arranged for Chen Bao's release, and for two strong, swift men to carry him home in a covered sedan chair.

He moved behind his desk, but did not sit down. He looked hard at me.

"Well, Old Boy, you did it this time," he said. He shook his head.

I nodded and kept my eyes locked on his.

"You're fired, Sun-jin. Give me your badge, warrant ID card, and your pistol. Leave the building immediately and don't return."

CHAPTER 80

I COULDN'T SLEEP THAT NIGHT. THE reality of what I'd done came home to me. I laid in bed, wide awake in the dark, listening to Bik grunt in her sleep and occasionally snort as if she was chasing something in a dream.

At about 4:00 a.m., I heard the creaking wheels of a rolling cart and the low-pitched singing of a man softly announcing his presence. It was the night-soil collector who had come to gather up the neighborhood's honey pots.

Only the night-soil collector has a job worse than mine was, I thought. *Well, maybe not worse than mine. He, at least, sells his collected excrement to farmers who use it as manure for their fruits and vegetables. That's more than I could do with all the shit I received at my job.*

I got out of bed at 5:00, fed Bik, filled her water bowl, then practiced my *Shaolin* Form. Bik stayed close to me the whole time I practiced, watching me. She then followed me from my practice area to the commode, then sat outside the tub as I showered.

She walked back to my bedroom with me and watched as I dressed. She seemed to sense I was upset.

At 11:00, when I left my flat, I patted her head, let her lick the back of my hand, and let her out the front door downstairs.

I went to see Sun-yu to tell him the news. I knew he would be both sad I had lost the job I loved, but also happy. That was the way of Eldest Brother. Always the good Taoist, always influenced by the complementary and conflicting Yin and Yang of life.

"You never were meant to be a policeman," Sun-yu said.

"Why's that?"

"You are too thoughtful, to introspective, but also too rigid to survive in a bureaucracy such as the SMP."

"I guess then I never would have survived as a member of one of the criminal triads," I responded. "They are the ultimate rigid bureaucracies." The irony of this remark was lost on Eldest Brother.

"What will you do now?"

"I haven't decided, but I am leaning toward becoming a private detective. I'll have to apply for a license, of course, and the Council might refuse to give it to me."

Sun-yu nodded.

We both knew the Council *would* reject my application, not *might* reject it. *Why couldn't I just admit that out loud and not do this silly dance with Eldest Brother?*

"You were right about one thing," I said.

"*Ayeeyah*," Sun-yu said. "Younger Brother finally admits that I was correct about something? What could that something possibly be?" He smiled.

"Life isn't just black vs. white, as I had thought, and had so conducted my life," I said, not looking Sun-yu in his eyes as I admitted this. "It is full of gray, ambiguous, often-changing areas. I accept that now."

Eldest Brother looked up toward the sky and said, as if to the heavens, "May the gods be praised. I was right after all."

I allowed his sarcasm to pass. "I'll tell you another thing. Life was easier for me when I saw it as all black vs. all white. Gray is much more difficult to manage."

Sun-yu nodded and put his hand on my shoulder. "Until you decide what you want to do, come work for me at the club. When you are ready, you will leave. I'll accept that when it occurs, with no hard feelings between us."

I was moved by Eldest Brother's gesture. "Thank you, Eldest Brother, but your club is not the life for me. I intend to continue in law enforcement."

"Of course you do," Sun-yu said, as he patted my shoulder and smiled. "So what will you do when the Council rejects your license application?"

"I will work in the shadows, as a detective without a license, taking only special cases — cases that a licensed private detective won't take because the powers-that-be might be offended."

"But when the Council rejects your license application, Sun-jin, as it surely will, how will you ever obtain a license to carry a revolver or pistol? The Council never will grant you that license, either, and this city is too dangerous for you to work in without a revolver or pistol."

"You will help me buy a weapon from one of your contacts. I will work as an unlicensed detective who carries an unlicensed, illegal revolver or pistol."

Sun-yu shook his head. He and I hugged once, and I left.

CHAPTER 81

A S I EXPECTED, MY APPLICATION to obtain a license to work as a private detective in the Settlement was rejected by the Council. The stated grounds were that I had been insubordinate as a policeman and had denigrated the SMP by my bad behavior — both true — and that I was incompetent to correctly conduct a proper investigation — clearly not true since I had solved the mystery of the deaths in the Flowery Kingdom. The rejection letter also said that I was likely to bring all law enforcement into disrepute if I were granted the license and allowed to work in law enforcement.

I took my time when this result occurred and, with Eldest Brother's help through his triad contacts, went out over the next several weeks and purchased several illegal revolvers and pistols. Then I put out the word through Eldest Brother and other nightclub owners that I was in business to handle *difficult* cases — cases that clients might not want known by the authorities. Approximately five weeks after I received the letter from the Council stating I would not receive a private investigator's license or a license to carry a revolver or pistol, I received my first case from a triad member.

———◦⬢◦———

Over the next few months, I noted several things, all of which indicated to me that I had finally taken the correct path in my life.

For one, the murders at the sporting houses had stopped. At least they no longer were reported in the newspapers. I suspected that they had ended.

Second, neither Taipan Sassoon nor Comprador Chen Bao was arrested and prosecuted for their roles in the sporting house murders. Again, that would have been in the newspapers had it occurred.

I also noted that neither the person who had made the offers to buy the sporting house properties, nor the other man who had committed the killings at the sporting houses was arrested. That didn't surprise me either. It followed naturally from the SMP's decision not to pursue Taipan Sassoon or his comprador.

I decided that Eldest Brother had been correct over the years when he used to say that if you had enough money, you then had power. And if you had sufficient power, you then had great influence. And if you had enough influence, then for you, crime could pay.

I dumped this thought and came back into my world. It was time for me to get to work on my first case so as not to anger the triad member who had sent it to me. For that would be bad *joss*.

THE END

ACKNOWLEDGEMENTS

First, of course, my thanks to Dominica who, as always, both encouraged me to write this book and then supported my efforts.

I am fortunate to have had several people who acted as my early readers — reading the manuscript before it was finalized and tearing into several parts of it, forcing me to re-think several scenes and chapters. You all improved my book. Since some of you have expressed your desire to remain anonymous, I won't name anybody. You know who you are, and you have my gratitude.

I also am fortunate to have a loyal group of readers I call my Launch Team. Each of you read the final manuscript in its final stage — after the early readers — and commented on it. You, too, all immensely improved my book. For that I am very grateful.

PLEASE REVIEW *DEATH IN THE FLOWERY KINGDOM* ON AMAZON

If you enjoyed **DEATH IN THE FLOWERY KINGDOM**, please post a review on Amazon at **www.Amazon.com**. Search for the book review page under my name or under its title, **DEATH IN THE FLOWERY KINGDOM.**

Reviews will help me, as an author, and also will help other readers decide if they want to read my book.

DOWNLOAD A FREE COPY *MANDARIN YELLOW*

The first Socrates Cheng mystery
Copy and paste this link into your browser or, if you are reading the page on a tablet or other digital device, click this link to download a free copy:
http://www.stevenmroth.com/FreeBook.aspx

Visit me at www.StevenMRoth.com to see all of my published books and receive information about my upcoming books

STEVEN M. ROTH

Steve, a retired lawyer, has written (i) a three-book mystery series featuring his Chinese/Greek/American private eye , Socrates Cheng, (ii) a two-book thriller/suspense series featuring an ex-Navy SEAL, Trace Austin, and, (iii) the first book, DEATH IN THE FLOWERY KINGDOM, in his new 1930s Shanghai, China, mystery series.

All of Steve's books have a solid and interesting historic and cultural aspect to their current-day plots, and all are well researched and developed to reflect these aspects of Steve's stories. The Socrates Cheng mystery series explores murder within the historical context of Socrates' Chinese heritage (MANDARIN YELLOW), within the historical context of Socrates' Greek heritage (THE MOURNING WOMAN), and in relationship to Socrates' interest in the Civil War and in Robert E. Lee (THE COUNTERFEIT TWIN).

Steve's suspense/thriller series (NO SAFE PLACE and NO PLACE TO HIDE), featuring ex-Navy SEAL Trace Austin, explores the plight of an individual and his family who are innocently caught-up in intrigues involving the abuse of Presidential power and home-grown biological-weapon terrorism in the United States.

Steve's new Shanghai murder mystery series is projected to comprise four or five books, and takes place in Shanghai, China, from 1935 until December 7, 1941, when the Japanese occupied and took control of Shanghai. The first book in the series (DEATH IN THE FLOWERY KINGDOM) involves murder, cultural clashes, and Shanghai's conflicting and confusing ambiance in 1935, all as experienced by Shanghai Municipal Police Inspector-Detective, Sun-jin.

Steve is currently writing the third Trace Austin suspense/thriller.

All of Steve's books and other information about him can be found on his web site at www.StevenMRoth.com.

Feel free to contact Steve at:
E-Mail: StevenMRoth_Author@comcast.net
Twitter: @StevenMRoth
Facebook: http://tinyurl.com/44c3bsp